DETOUR
HELEN NIELSEN

Black Lizard Books
Berkeley • 1988

Helen Nielsen was born in Roseville, Illinois, in 1918. She worked in Chicago and Los Angeles as a free-lance commercial artist and a draftsman, as well as an aero-engineer. She began writing novels in 1951, the best-known of which are **Sing Me A Murder** and **Detour**. She lives in Southern California.

PS
3564
I35
D4
1988

INTRODUCTION

By Marcia Muller

In the 1950s a proliferation of male-oriented digest-sized mystery and detective magazines provided an on-the-job training ground for such writers as Evan Hunter (Ed McBain), Harry Whittington, John Jakes, and Gil Brewer. While earning a living, they also learned how to create the clean economical prose, fast-moving action scenes, and crisp dialogue that to this day are staples of good suspense writing.

Owing to the predominantly male themes and subject matter of such magazines as *Manhunt*, *Accused*, *Hunted*, *Pursuit*, and *Justice*, few of the contributors were women; but those who did break into the market were very good indeed. Of a group whose members include Craig Rice, Pat Stadley, and De Forbes (Stanton Forbes), Helen Nielsen went on to apply the exacting techniques of magazine fiction to the creation of such highly suspenseful, richly complex and critically acclaimed novels as *Detour* and *Sing Me a Murder*.

Nielsen's novels in no way fit the definition of hardboiled or *noir* fiction as epitomized by other authors represented in the Black Lizard line (Jim Thompson and Paul Cain, for example). Her work is too emotional and we are too privy to the thoughts and feelings of her characters for the books to be classified as such. They are better termed realistic fiction: Uncompromising in their faithful depiction of the world as it is—or *could* be, had her characters actually lived and the events described by her actually occurred.

Nielsen's primary theme is that of a profound quest by her protagonist: Danny Ross, hero of *Detour*, is fleeing the United States for Mexico, not "running away from life . . . running toward it;" in the process he is forced to seek the truth about the dangerous events in which he has unwittingly become embroiled. Ty Leander, protagonist of *Sing Me a Murder*, initially appears—in his suicide attempt—to be seeking death; next we feel he is seeking to absolve another man of murder; finally his motives and aims are proven to be far more complex than either of these.

Nielsen's characters, such as Danny and Ty, are multi-dimensional, believably motivated, and—like most of us—not always wholly consistent. Her descriptions of them are deft—saying a great deal in few words, as in her introduction of Ty Leander:

> He was a young man, awkwardly tall. His eyes were set deep under heavy brows, his dark hair tumbled about on his head as if long uncombed by anything other than an occasional thrust of nervous fingers. His imported tweed suit nagged at his shoulders; he would always appear to be outgrowing his clothes no matter how expensive the tailoring.

This tells us all we need to know about Ty on first impression—until his puzzling actions raise questions that make us read on, seeking explanations.

The explanations are buried deep in an intricately wrought plot, and Nielsen cleverly leads us to many false conclusions before she reveals the true one. Her plots are as inventive and deceptive as any classic puzzler; we are given enough information and clues so that—however surprising the solution—we find it to be the logical conclusion of the preceding action. (This plotting ability stood Nielsen in good stead as a scriptwriter for such high quality '50s and '60s television shows as *Perry Mason*, *Alfred Hitchcock Presents*, *Alcoa Theatre*, and *87th Precinct*.) And while much of this action is violent, Nielsen neither shrinks from it nor dwells upon it in unnecessary detail. Realism again. The world in which her stories take place is clearly recognizable and never sentimentalized.

Reading a Nielsen novel—in particular *Detour* or *Sing Me a Murder*—is never wholly an escape; our identification with her people, fear for their safety, and hopes for their futures is too strong for that. On the other hand, her work is always stimulating because it hones the senses and heightens our awareness of the world as we know it.

At a time when more and more women writers are receiving long overdue recognition for their realistic and hard-hitting suspense fiction, the reissue of these books is especially fitting. I, for one, am delighted to see them back in print—and I hope many new readers will discover Helen Nielsen, as I was once so fortunate to do. As respected critic Anthony Boucher said of *Sing Me a Murder*, her work is "opulent with unpredictable pleasure."

Marcia Muller
Sonoma, California
June 29, 1987

Chapter One

Danny didn't want to hitch a ride with the old man, but it was hot walking in the sun and no telling how far it might be to the next town. This was a lonely country he'd come to, a flat, arid corridor between twin ranges of low mountains that swelled up like calluses on the hand of God. Danny had come a long way from Chicago, and he still had a long way to go.

Until the universal gave out back at the foot of the last pass, he'd been making pretty good time—in spite of the fuel pump, the radiator, and a few other ailments a seventeen-year-old jalopy can develop on the road; but being on foot wasn't so bad now that the mountains were leveling out and the border was getting nearer all the time. As for the jalopy, he'd meant to ditch it before crossing into Mexico anyway. A hundred miles or so, one way or the other, didn't make much difference.

Danny Ross was taking no chances. He'd spent a long time planning this migration, and it was going to be done right. That's why he'd kept to the lonely roads instead of the main highways, and that's why the car had to roll over the grade into the ditch. Disappeared without trace—that's what was happening to Danny Ross. He was just going to walk right off the face of the earth so far as the old ties were concerned, and none of the ties were very old because Danny was barely eighteen. Eighteen and skinny in a pair of tight levis and an old leather jacket, with his sun-bleached hair cut a quick two inches from his scalp, and his tanned face marked with anger and pride. Danny wasn't running away from life; he was running toward it. Nobody was going to cage him! While he walked, he pulled a well-thumbed language dictionary from a canvas zipper bag (Danny believed in traveling light) and took up his studies

1

where he'd left off last. And then an old man drove up in a dusty sedan and held open the door.

"Ride, son?"

Danny closed the book and sized up the source of this offer. The old man looked harmless enough. His face was like a pink and yellow apple just beginning to wither, and his eyes were a blue that time had faded to the shade of old denim. This was the first car to come along in almost an hour, and there was no reason, Danny decided, to walk when he could ride. Having won the decision, he shoved the book into his pocket and climbed into the front seat.

The worst part of a hitch was always the conversation. "Going far?" the old man asked, just as Danny knew he would, and Danny shrugged. "A ways," he said.

"Pretty hot walking."

Sure it was hot walking. It was hot in the sedan, too, with the sun, dipping a little to the west, pouring in through Danny's window, and with a sickish odor in the car that made him a little dizzy. He looked around to find a place for his zipper bag, and that's when he saw the little black satchel on the back seat. It had gold lettering on it: Chas. W. Gaynor, M.D.

M.D. That was a good racket, a hellova lot better than doctoring motors in some smelly garage, but the old man didn't look so flush. The collar of the alpaca jacket creeping up about his scrawny neck was frayed at the fold, and his Panama hat had yellowed with age. And the sedan! Danny listened to the motor and shook his head. This baby was due for either a rebore or a nice, deep ditch like the jalopy! People must be pretty healthy in this country if the doc was any indication.

"You're not a local boy," the doctor remarked. "I've been practicing in this country for fifty years. I'd know you or some of your kinfolk if you were."

"No," Danny admitted. "I'm just bumming around, seeing the country." (Nobody was going to get anything out of him.)

"That's a fine idea. I remember planning something of the sort when I was a lad. I was going to see faraway lands and strange people. Somehow my plans just didn't work out."

2

Danny was thinking how the doc had been young a little too soon. Nowadays you could travel to faraway lands without making plans; the plans were all made for you. But he kept his mouth shut and hoped the conversation was over. Queer old duck, the doc. Now he seemed to have forgotten all about his newly acquired passenger. His long hands gripped the steering wheel until the veins etched blue against the ivory skin; but the road was still smooth and empty of traffic, except for a pair of saddle horses ambling single file along the soft, unfenced shoulder. For a moment Danny feared he might be sick, but then the grip on the wheel eased, and the old man returned from his woolgathering.

"Faraway lands and strange people," he repeated. "And none stranger than ourselves. . . . But what have we here? Spanish-English Dictionary—My, you are a studious young man!"

Danny made a grab for the book, which had slipped out of his jacket pocket. It really didn't matter if the old man saw what it was, but if anybody started looking for Danny Ross one of these days and traced him this far, some old guy remembering he'd been studying Spanish could give them a good lead. "I found it," he lied quickly. "I was just looking it over. It doesn't hurt a guy to know another language."

"No, it doesn't," the doctor agreed. "Sometimes I wish that I knew another language. Some special language that would make it easy to say the things we don't want to say. Did you ever think how strange it is that with all the tongues of men, all the arts, all the modern inventions, it is still so very difficult for two people sitting in the same room to communicate with one another?"

Danny gave the doctor a sidelong glance and then settled back against the seat cushion. So he was off again. A nut, maybe, but what difference did it make so long as the sedan kept rolling south? And then Danny closed his eyes, because, nutty or not, from here on the doc could communicate with himself.

It was the vibration of the wheels leaving the pavement that put an end to Danny's nap. He might have dozed five minutes, or even half an hour, but the sun was still there

3

when he opened his eyes, and the desert, and a stack of ugly yellow buildings piled up at the crossing of an unpaved road. Danny caught a glimpse of the name on the canopy over the gas pumps as the doc drove around back to park in the shade of the buildings: Mountain View. In this country that could mean a gas station, a country store, or even a whole town all under one roof.

"Sorry to disturb your sleep," the old man said, switching off the ignition, "but I always stop in here when I'm on the road. Sometimes I'm needed and folks leave word. I'm a doctor."

This was no news to Danny. He answered by reaching for his canvas bag.

"Oh, there's no need for that," the doctor added quickly. "I'll be going on to Cooperton in a few minutes. If you want to ride that far, just sit tight. Or better yet, come on in with me, and we'll have a cold drink."

Cooperton was a little black dot on the map Danny carried folded up in his hip pocket, and it was still farther south, so that was fine. But the cold drink sounded fine, too, and he didn't need a second invitation to follow the doctor inside. He'd been right about Mountain View. It was one of those all purpose stops: service station, garage, café—even a grocery counter off to the left side as they came through the sighing screen door. On the opposite wall was a counter with a row of stools, all empty but one, where a plump young woman with greasy hair was opening a beer for her only customer. The customer was a man, small and wiry, who was wearing a soiled canvas hat and a wrinkled trench coat that looked pretty silly in all this sunshine—until you noticed the already overpacked Gladstone at his feet. Yes, Mountain View was also the depot for the local bus line.

"Evening, Walter—Rice. And how are you today, Viola?"

It was still a long way from evening by Danny's watch, but this was the doctor's way of greeting his friends. First the balding young man behind the grocery counter, then his lanky, Stetson-crowned customer, and finally the woman who had now finished opening the beer and was wiping off counter space for the newcomers. With the exception of a couple of Indian boys squatting on their heels outside the door, this comprised the entire current population of Mountain View.

"How am I always?" Viola responded to the question. "Healthy as a horse—you know me."

They were going to go on trading sharp dialogue like that for a while, and Danny wasn't interested. He climbed onto one of the stools and gazed longingly at his neighbor's beer, but there was a sign on the wall prohibiting the sale of intoxicants to minors, and considering the way the old man kept babying him a break didn't seem likely. "Coke," he muttered, when the big-breasted woman finally got around to asking what he wanted. In a moment she was back from the ice chest with a pair of frosted bottles.

Two dime drinks and her work was over, but she didn't move away. She made a halfhearted swipe at one of the blue-tailed flies buzzing about her head without even looking at it; she only had eyes for the old man.

"We heard about Francy," she began at last. "Somebody said they got a call from Red Rock at the mortuary."

"Somebody said!"

The subject didn't sound humorous to Danny, but it seemed to amuse the tall man in the Stetson. He came across the room in a couple of elongated strides to horn in on the conversation. "I'll bet Viola had her ear glued to the party line all morning," he chuckled. "How about it, Charley?"

"Do you think that's all I have to do around here?" Viola wailed. "If you must know it was that shiftless husband of mine who told me! Ask him where he heard it."

The party was getting real cozy now, with everybody crowded around the doctor's sagging shoulders like a bevy of matrons hot on the trail of a risqué rumor. Danny couldn't have helped overhearing what was said.

"I heard she never did regain consciousness," the balding Walter remarked. "I don't suppose we'll ever know what happened."

"Like as not Francy never knew either, the way she was liquored up."

The tall man—that was Rice, Danny remembered—was sure having a good time. He finished off that observation with a high-pitched laugh that just sort of faded away when the doctor raised his head. It was the first sign that the old

5

man was even listening to all that talk around him.

"Liquored up?" he echoed. "Did you see Francy last night, Rice?"

Rice hesitated. From the word "mortuary" Danny had been following the conversation like a spectator at the tennis matches. He saw Viola's troubled frown, Walter's anxious eyes, and the first sign of consternation on the face of the tall man.

"I guess I did," he admitted. "Sure, it was last night. I was having dinner with a cattle buyer at the Pioneer Hotel, and Francy was hanging around the bar as usual. Hell, Charley, you know as well as I do that girl ain't been cold sober since she left high school. What happened last night was bound to happen one way or another. Women like Francy Allen don't die of old age!"

Rice looked about him in search of confirmation; but although he'd made Francy sound very interesting, Viola had other ideas. "Maybe not!" she snapped. "I'm not an expert on women like Francy, but I'd still like to know what happened on the road last night. You can't just find a woman lying unconscious in her own blood and shrug it off. Maybe Francy was hit by a car, or maybe she smashed her own head that way, but you'll have to prove it to me!"

"Now, baby," Walter interrupted, "don't go making mountains out of molehills—"

"Molehills! This is no molehill! What if it wasn't an accident? If there's someone on the loose around here who does things like that to women, something should be done about it!"

Silence drew a heavy frame around Viola's outburst. Nobody had a thing to say until the doctor pushed aside his untouched drink and came to his feet.

"Yes," he said quietly, "something should be done about it. . . . Any calls for me, Walter?"

It took a moment for Walter to come out of his trance. "Not a call," he said. "We're all too healthy, I guess. . . . But you can drop around in another six months." A nervous laugh and a quick pat on his wife's sweaty cheek didn't do much to ease the tension. Just as Danny had thought in the beginning, Francy wasn't a humorous subject.

"Then there's no reason for me to hang around here any

6

longer," the doctor concluded. "No, finish your drink, son," he added, as Danny attempted to rise. "I want to check the radiator anyway. Use a lot of water in weather like this."

Danny would just as soon have gone along with the old man then, but something in that grave face told him he wasn't wanted. The old man was troubled; he preferred to be alone. But he wasn't too troubled to forget something Rice had said. Two steps toward the door, and he turned back again, almost smiling. "By the way," he remarked, "did you sell that buyer any cattle?"

The way Rice's ears reddened was a dead giveaway that he'd been caught off base. "Well, yes, I did," he admitted. "Of course prices aren't as good as I'd hoped—"

"They never are," the doctor murmured.

"Oh, I'm going to pay up, Charley. It's been a long time, but I haven't forgotten you. As a matter of fact, I was hoping you'd stop by. I might as well give it to you now as put it in the bank. Never stays there long anyway."

While he reached for words, Rice was also reaching for a hip pocket that yielded a wallet of astonishing thickness. Danny didn't mean to stare, but he couldn't pry his eyes away from all that beautiful currency. This boy was loaded! Now he was peeling off twenties as if they were petals on a daisy.

"One sixty, one eighty, two hundred. There, I guess that squares us. Christ, but it's expensive to have a sick wife!"

"Funerals are expensive too," the doctor murmured. "And remember what I told you. Mrs. Rice needs plenty of rest and peace of mind."

That was a nice prescription the old man handed out; Danny could have used some of that himself. He also could have used that fistful of money in the old man's hand. Not that Danny was destitute, but money was something he'd never had enough of. He watched, fascinated, while the doctor extracted a long leather wallet from the inner pocket of his alpaca jacket. When a folded sheet of white paper slipped from the wallet and floated lazily to the floor, Danny was after it instantly. But instantly wasn't fast enough. The man in the wrinkled raincoat was a spectator to this event too, and he moved a lot faster than Danny.

"You dropped something, doc," he said, and the old man

7

thanked him vaguely and put the paper away with the money. He was stuffing the wallet into the inner pocket again as he went out the door.

Danny had his cue. He dawdled over the Coke so the old man would have time to get hold of himself. No wonder he seemed so upset if he'd just lost a patient like this lady called Francy. Danny's mouth twisted into an offside grin. What a choice item for these hicks to buzz about! And nothing to it, most likely. Just anything to brighten a dull life. But Danny had another kind of life to think about now, and all of this was nothing to him. He began thinking of what was ahead, what he'd do once he'd crossed the border into freedom. There was that friend of his who'd gone to Mexico City—he could look him up for a starter. After that, who could tell? Move on south maybe. Central America—South America. Anywhere was all right with Danny just so long as it wasn't back home, because home was a big trap they were getting set to spring on Danny Ross—only Danny had other plans.

"I sure hope that bus is on time."

That was the man in the raincoat busting in on Danny's daydreams.

"It usually is," Viola said, "unless they have trouble on the road. It'll be along any minute now."

"It can't come too soon for me!"

Danny knew just how the man felt when he paid for the beer and started pacing back and forth to the screen door. A few minutes could be a long time in this Godforsaken spot, and this boy was no local yokel—not with that quick, nervous step and those anxious eyes. The proof came when he relaxed long enough to slip a coin into the juke box by the door, and let up a howl at the first wail of the fiddles. "Hillbillies!" he stormed. "That's all you have in this country, hillbillies and cowboys! Didn't anybody ever hear of Louis Prima?"

"You don't have to play it," Viola shrugged.

"And I don't have to listen!" Distaste made a wrinkled monkey face under that soiled canvas hat, and the man came back to the counter and grabbed his suitcase. "Maybe I've got time to wash up," he suggested. "Where's the men's room?"

8

"Outside and around to your left. And don't hurry back!" Viola called.

It was peculiar how lonely Danny began to feel when he was left at the counter all alone. The man in the raincoat might not be such a pleasant character, but he wasn't nearly as strange as these sun-browned people with the high cheekbones and the tired drawls. Did they all have to be so tall? Danny hadn't filled out yet, but he'd never thought of himself as being puny until he'd sat there at the counter surrounded by the giant named Rice, and the balding Walter, and that buxom Amazon with the oily hair. Even the old doctor was tall and spare, like a ragged pine tree that stands alone. Danny had a longing to ask the man in the raincoat where he was from, and if he knew the Blackhawk or the Chez Paree. Not that Danny was an expert, but he could talk like one to a stranger.

Rice finished his business and went out, and the fiddles stopped wailing in the juke box. Now the place was silent and empty because Viola had gone back to the kitchen with the dirty glasses, and Walter was in the stock room. The doctor had paid for the drinks, which was fair enough considering all the uses Danny had for his own bank roll, and nobody said, "Good-by," or "Come again," when he left the café.

The Indian boys were still squatting in the shade of the canopy outside, and up the road, the very road Danny had just traveled, came a fat yellow bus with its left-turn signal out and its hoarse horn making salutation. It was a southbound bus and that gave Danny an idea. Maybe it was being so close to the border that made him uneasy, but suddenly he couldn't wait any longer. He couldn't chance another hitch at Cooperton, or waste another couple of days riding shanks' mare. Cough up the fare and get rolling—that was the answer.

But just as he decided to hop aboard, Danny remembered the zipper bag on the back seat of the doctor's sedan. It was only a short sprint away—he could still make it if he hurried. Rounding the corner of the building, he ran headlong into the man with the raincoat, bag in hand and coattails flying. There was a boy who wasn't going to miss his bus!

"Tell 'em to wait for me," Danny yelled, and kept on running.

The sedan was still where the doctor had parked it—at the rear of the café in the shade of an outbuilding. Its dust-streaked hood was propped up, and the old man's jacket dangling from the spotlight indicated a man at work. Danny jerked open the back door and grabbed his bag.

"I've decided to take the bus," he called out. "Thanks for the ride."

There was no answer. Maybe the old man couldn't hear with his head under the hood, and it wouldn't be right to chase off and leave him waiting for a passenger who wasn't going to show. "I'm taking the bus," Danny repeated, coming around to the front of the sedan, "and thanks—"

He didn't get any further. Doctor Gaynor was there all right, slumped over the radiator with the screw cap still clutched in one hand; but that wasn't water dripping down on the cylinder head. It was blood.

Chapter Two

It was more blood than Danny had ever seen in his life. Once back home, when he was just a kid, he'd heard the grownups talking about someone who hemorrhaged to death, and for a moment he thought that was what had happened to the old man. But it didn't take more than a quick-second look to set that straight. The doctor had been checking the radiator all right, but something had hit him from behind—something hard and deadly that crushed his skull and started that red fountain flowing. There was a rock on the ground with the same red stain, and when Danny stooped to touch it, it was still sticky. He turned about quickly and sank to the ground as his knees gave out.

Back under the canopy, about a thousand miles away, there were sounds of living things and a throbbing motor, sounds filtered through the distance of from here to hereafter. A horn sounded, an engine roared, and the yellow bus kicked up a cloud of dust and gravel as it headed back onto the black top, but Danny was helpless to move or cry out. He knelt with his hands over his face, unmindful of the blood. The old man—the poor old man! After a few moments he remembered that something must be done.

Danny staggered to his feet and looked about wildly. The back door to the café was less than twenty feet away, but a sound in the opposite direction pulled him back. The sound of another motor, not the bus this time, was somewhere in the distance. He ran toward the crossroad and looked in both directions, but sound could be deceiving in this country and so could sight. Was that really a cloud of dust curling against the far horizon, or was it a trick of the heat? Was it the wake of a fleeing automobile, or the work of the wanton wind? There was no use examining the earth for tracks. The soil was hard and desert-dry, and the turnoff from the side road to that cluster of yellow buildings was strewn with rocks and gravel. But Danny had heard a motor. His ear was tuned for such a sound.

But now everything was as quiet. As far as the eye could reach there was nothing moving, nothing to be seen that had life or power of death. Just the two roads, one dirt and one black top, the desert, the mountains and behind him the frame shacks of the country store. There was an old shed near the sedan, and Danny looked behind it. A car could have parked there without being seen, but there were too many tracks to tell the story. By this time Danny was getting his bearings. The numbness and nausea had worn off, and there was nothing to do but go back to the café and tell the man and woman what had happened. He didn't have a doubt but what the old man was dead, but somebody else would have to make sure. Danny's legs were still shaking.

From the moment he turned the corner of the shed, Danny's world went crazy. It started with a scream, a wild, terrified scream that should have warned him if his imagination hadn't been limited for anything so fantastic. He took another step forward and the scream came again, but this time with words that stopped him in his tracks.

"There he is! My God, look at him! Look at the blood!"

It was the woman Viola who stood beside the old man's body screaming out her terror, but she wasn't looking at him. She was looking straight at Danny.

"Walter, look out! He'll kill you too!"

Had the woman gone mad? No wonder, in view of what she'd found, but what of her husband who came charging

11

out of the café's back door with a shotgun in his hand?

"Stop where you are!" he cried. "Don't move or I'll blow your head off!"

"Wait a minute—" Danny began.

"Don't move!"

Walter's voice had turned soprano, but there was nothing effeminate about that shotgun. "Go inside and call the sheriff," he commanded his wife. "I've got him covered."

At that instant Danny's fear was born. It was too horrible, too incredible to be true, and yet there he stood, straddle-legged and numb, with the old man's blood smeared on his face and hands, and a wild-eyed captor pointing a gun at his chest.

"You're crazy!" he cried. "I didn't kill the old man! He was like that when I found him!"

Danny might just as well have shouted at the sky.

The party line to Cooperton had been humming all day. Every rumor, every tale, every bit of gossip about Francy Allen had gone racing over that wire, and Francy was vulnerable. Francy was extremely vulnerable. But the frantic call from Mountain View struck like a bolt of lightning. It struck Ada Keep first of all.

"Virgil ain't in just now," she parrotted into the mouthpiece, and then stood transfixed while the woman on the other end of the wire poured out her grisly tale. Dr. Gaynor? Old Charley Gaynor? Viola had to repeat the message before Ada understood. "Virgil ain't in," she murmured weakly. "I'll send somebody to fetch him."

Ada Keep placed the receiver back on the hook and stared dumbly at the silent instrument. Then the tears began to well up in her small brown eyes and followed the wrinkle lines down her unpainted cheeks. It didn't seem possible! Why only yesterday—Ada brushed a wisp of graying hair from her forehead with a nervous hand and smiled crookedly. Three months, he had said. Three months, and now he was gone without any time at all. The Lord moved in strange and terrible ways.

And the news moved. Like the tumbleweed before the wind it rolled across town, floating up from the street to Dr. Glenn's new office over the Cattleman's Bank; racing down to an old frame house where a pale young woman listened from the wide front porch and gripped the railing with trembling hands; and finding Trace Cooper at his usual habitat in the bar of the Pioneer Hotel. Fifteen minutes after the call, Sheriff Virgil Keep stalked into his office to verify a rumor.

"Did you have to blab the whole story?" he raged. "Can't you take a message without stirring up the whole town?"

Ada wouldn't have thought of a defense even if her husband had time to listen. She'd been trying for thirty years.

But Virgil didn't have time for anything now but making fast tracks. Moments later he and his young deputy were racing toward Mountain View, leaving a shocked and murmuring town behind them. Folks were going to take the old man's death hard, especially since it came so close on the heels of that messy business last night. Two violent deaths in succession could put a strain on anyone's nerves.

Danny was inside the café when the sheriff's car pulled up at the door. He was sitting on one of the stools again with his hands spread out on the counter before him, and Walter's shotgun pointed at his head. No cold drinks were being served this time, and the juke box was silent; but even those wailing fiddles would have been easier to take than Viola's periodic sobs. The sound of wheels on the gravel was welcome. There was no use trying to tell these people anything! Surely the police would listen to reason.

The screen door opened, and two men came in. One was just an ordinary man with an ordinary man's face, but the sight of the other made Danny's throat go dry. It wasn't just his size, although he was built like an all-star tackle; it was that terrible anger in his eyes.

Virgil Keep looked at Danny, at Walter's gun, and at the woman huddled against the ice chest. Then without any preliminaries he went to work.

"Where's the body?" he demanded.

Walter nodded toward the door. "Around the left side—clear back to the shed. You'll see Charley's car."

The two men went out together, the sheriff and the deputy. They were dressed alike—suntan cotton twill pants and shirts and wide-brimmed hats; but nobody had to tell

Danny which was which. The big man carried his authority like a battle flag. And he was much more than just a cow-country sheriff; he was doom come to catch up with Danny Ross. The devil he'd been fleeing all his life until at last he couldn't run any farther.

When the men came back the deputy looked sick, but nothing could alter the expression or color of Virgil Keep. He went straight to the phone, and Danny could hear him speaking the words with no more emotion than if he'd been ordering a snack from the corner drugstore.

"Hello, Tom? This is Virgil Keep. Did your ambulance get back from Red Rock yet? . . . Good. We need it out here at Walter Wade's place. Hurry up and keep your mouth shut."

The receiver went back on the hook, and Virgil returned to the center of the room. "Waste of time telling Tom to keep his mouth shut," he muttered. "It's all over town that Charley Gaynor's been murdered. They're even saying you people caught the killer in the act. How about that?"

The question was for Walter. "Well, not exactly," he said. "But he was the only one around—and he came in with the doctor."

"That's what I thought. The fool woman never got anything straight in her life!"

Virgil came and stood before Danny, and his eyes, dark and penetrating under heavy brows, were taking inventory of the bloody face and bloody hands. But they were doing more than that. They were measuring just how weak Danny Ross could be. They were following the line of his mouth, the lower lip bulging just a little, and the cut of the chin that wouldn't hold steady.

"What have you got to say for yourself?" he demanded, and Danny could have foretold the question word for word.

"I didn't kill the old man," Danny said. "I found him that way."

Not a flicker of sympathy in those eyes. Just that knifelike stare.

"Where'd you get all that blood?"

"From him. From the rock, I guess. I don't remember. I was sick."

"Why didn't you call for help?"

14

"I couldn't. I couldn't make a sound."

"You could move, couldn't you?"

"He could move, all right!" Walter sputtered. "He was trying to run away!"

"I wasn't running away! I was coming back!"

Danny felt dizzy. He wanted a drink of water, but nobody was going to give it to him even if he asked. He had to explain, somehow, and it wasn't easy when he didn't understand himself. He had to take them back with him through that awful time when he stepped around to the front of the sedan and found the old man dead. He had to make them feel the shock and the nausea, and make them hear the yellow bus leaving and then the other sound.

"I thought I heard a car pulling away," he stammered. "I ran to see."

"Where did you run?"

"To the crossroads. I looked both ways. I think there was a dust cloud off that way."

Danny waved one arm heedless of directions.

"But you didn't see the car?" the sheriff asked.

"No, I didn't see a car. So I came back and looked for tracks. That's what I was doing behind the shed."

"Don't you believe him!" Viola cried out. "I saw him when he came around that shed, and I saw his face. It was the face of a killer!"

"Honey, take it easy," Walter began, but he was wasting his breath. All this time the woman had been half hidden behind the counter, but not for a moment had her sharp eyes left Danny's face, and not for an instant had her mind stopped working. "Look at him!" she cried. "Can't you see what he is? A no-good bum, a tramp the doctor picked up on the road! A hitchhiker!"

"There's no law against that," the deputy said.

"And no law against what happened to the doctor? Or what happened to Francy Allen?"

The sudden silence was worse than Viola's screaming. It was like the unveiling of a painting, or the raising of a baton before the downbeat. Francy. The name lit a candle in every eye.

"What do you mean?" Virgil demanded.

"What do you think I mean?" the woman cried. "They

15

died the same way, didn't they? I knew it wasn't an accident. How could it be an accident? Drunk or sober, how could Francy give herself a brain concussion if she was walking alone on the highway?"

"Wait a minute!" Danny yelled. "I wasn't even near here last night!"

"That's what you say!"

It was the sheriff who finally got Viola to shut up. He'd come out here because old Charley Gaynor was dead—she could kindly leave Francy out of this. "It's her condition," Walter explained. "She gets so excited over things." But Virgil Keep wasn't interested in any woman's condition; he wanted facts. From Walter he would get them, not so eloquently or dramatically as from Viola, but with considerably more accuracy.

His wife had discovered the body when she stepped outside the kitchen door to add a few bottles to the crate of empties on the porch. Her cries brought him running with his gun, and he saw the boy, this Danny Ross as he called himself, standing over the old man. Sure he recognized him. Charley had brought him in for a Coke not fifteen minutes earlier. Charley was always picking up people on the road.

"Was the boy running away?" Virgil asked.

"No," Walter admitted, "he wasn't running anywhere. He was walking toward the café."

For the first time since Virgil Keep walked into the room, Danny began to relax. There, you see, he told himself, it's all going to work out after all. It's nothing but a crazy mistake because a woman became frightened and a man had a gun in his hand. In a few minutes everything would be straightened out, and Danny Ross would be on his way. Confidence gave him a voice.

"That's what I told you," he said. "I didn't kill the old man. Would I come back here if I had? He gave me a lift, that's all. I had no reason to kill him."

"No reason!"

They could silence Viola for just so long, but now she was back again, her sweaty face leaning toward Danny's and her heavy breasts heaving with emotion. "What about that two hundred dollars?" she cried. "Listen to me, Virgil

Keep. Charley had two hundred dollars. We both saw it, both Walter and me. He stood right where you're standing now and took the money off Jim Rice—Jim still owed for Ethel's operation—and all the time this young hoodlum sat there watching. You should have seen his eyes!"

Nobody could deny Viola now. She pulled out an object from under the counter, and Danny's heart stood still. It was the old man's threadbare coat, limp and empty.

"We all saw Charley put the money in this coat, but it's not there now! Ask him! Ask this young tramp what he did with Charley's wallet!"

It was then that doom came in and met Danny Ross. The sheriff could send his deputy out to search the old man's body, but Danny didn't need his report to know the wallet was gone. Now Danny even knew where and how it had gone, but these people wouldn't believe him. They'd never believe him after the sheriff's big ham hands ripped into his pockets. He was just a down and out hitchhiker without the price of a cold drink until the contents of his billfold was dumped out on the counter. The small bills and chicken feed didn't count. The big stuff was enough. . . . One sixty, one eighty, two hundred.

"All right," the sheriff said. "Let's go."

Chapter Three

Cooperton was a little town, and the same things happen in little towns as in big cities—only not so often. Babies are born, lovers marry (and sometimes don't), and old men die. But Charley Gaynor wasn't just any old man, and he hadn't died in bed. Charley was like the town square, or the flag flying over the Post Office. He was the war memorial plaque at the Town Hall (most of those names were boys Charley had delivered) and the little white sign at the edge of town that read: Cooperton, pop. 997. Charley Gaynor belonged to Cooperton, and so, in quite another way, would his slayer.

Danny could feel the tension in the streets as soon as they pulled up to the sheriff's station. He'd gotten his ride to

Cooperton after all, a fast, easy ride in a smooth-running sedan with an emblem painted on the door; but he hadn't noticed how the motor sang or how the shock absorbers took the dips. It was a short ride, ten miles by the meter on the dashboard, and a couple of miles beyond Mountain View the sheriff slowed down a bit and seemed to be watching Danny's face as they passed an angling side road that forked in out of a pass through the hills. Danny trembled without knowing why.

But in Cooperton he knew why. The streets weren't exactly crowded, but they were busy. They whispered as the sedan drove by, and they murmured when it parked. And then down the highway behind them came the racing ambulance with its silly siren clearing the way for an old man who wasn't in a hurry any more.

"Get along inside," the sheriff said, and Danny didn't need a second invitation.

The sheriff's office was the front room of a long, flat-roofed building that served the disciplinary needs of the community. Behind the office a short hall led to a few cells for the overnight guests (seldom used unless the boys got too free with their bottles), and the rest of the building was given over to the simple living quarters of the sheriff and his wife. There was the smell of frying food coming from someplace beyond that hall, and then a scrawny little woman in a long percale apron appeared in the doorway with a bread knife in her hand. Maybe the knife was accident, but Danny couldn't help feeling the woman was disappointed when she looked at him. She wiped her free hand on the apron skirt and murmured:

"Why, he's just a boy!"

They were the first words Danny heard from Ada Keep, and they were sad and regretful like her eyes.

Virgil shoved a straight-backed oak chair at Danny and muttered a terse, "Sit down." Then he went back to lock the front door against the group of curious spectators already clustered about the entrance. "Go on home and eat your suppers," he said. "There's nothing you can do here." Maybe that would send them away, maybe not. Virgil didn't much care, because with that bolt shot home he wasn't going to be disturbed anyway. Danny watched the whole procedure with unbelieving eyes. It couldn't be true. In a minute he'd come out of this nightmare and stop sweating, but in the meantime that giant in the suntan twills had shoved the wide-brimmed hat on the back of his head and was telephoning a man named Jim Rice. Rice drifted into focus again—the tall man with the too easy laugh.

"You did? Two hundred. Yes, that's what Walter said." The sheriff was talking about that money again, and Danny was at the edge of his chair. "All right," Virgil finished. "That's what I wanted to know. You'd better get down here right away, Jim, and see if you can identify that money."

"How can he identify my money?" Danny screamed. "It's my money! I've been trying to tell you, it's my money!"

Virgil hung up the phone and sat down behind his desk. He pulled Danny's billfold out of his pocket and dumped the contents on the table top. It came to about two hundred and seven dollars altogether—money sure didn't last long on the road. There were a few other things too. A driver's license, a couple of snapshots of cute, empty-faced girls, a social security card.

"I worked for that money," Danny said. "I worked in a garage . . . after school, Saturdays, Sundays. When school was out I worked all day."

"And saved your pay," Virgil added. He'd heard all this before.

"I saved what I could."

"You didn't spend it on these pretty girls?"

"What girls? They don't mean anything."

"Vernon Halsey works in Claymore's garage," Ada said eagerly. "I don't reckon he's any older than this boy."

Ada always sounded excited when she spoke, as if speech was a new art she had just mastered and was showing off. But the eagerness in her face faded as Virgil raised his head. It was wrong again. Everything she said was always wrong.

"Why aren't you getting supper?" he demanded, and she began backing toward the hallway.

"I just wanted to know about the doctor—"

"You know about the doctor! Thanks to your big mouth the whole town knows about the doctor, and if they come down here and take this prisoner away from me you can be thanked for that, too!"

"But they wouldn't do that! Why would anybody do that?"

Danny didn't need an answer. He'd felt it in the street. He was a stranger in the midst of a hostile people. The whole world had suddenly gone crazy, nothing would surprise him now. And then, while Ada stood there with one red hand clasping her own throat and that long bread knife dangling from another, somebody began to rattle the doorknob and kick against the door. The timing was perfect. Danny's face turned as pale as skim milk.

"Hey, Virgil, what the hell's the idea?"

It was the deputy again. They'd left him back at Mountain View to ride in with the body in the ambulance, and now Virgil had to unlock the door and let him in. Another man was with him, a man not so young as the deputy and not so old as the sheriff. He had the white skin of an indoors man and the clothes of somebody who doesn't worry about paying the rent.

"Doctor Glenn was at the mortuary when we drove in," the deputy explained. "He examined the wound—"

"Not examined," the doctor corrected. "Just a quick look. It'll take time for an autopsy. Messy business."

"Real messy," Virgil agreed. "What about the rock?"

The deputy had the rock in his hand. It was wrapped up in newspaper now, but there were stains coming through and a rough, jagged edge that poked up from the parcel when he placed it on the sheriff's desk.

"Apparently that was the weapon," Doctor Glenn said. "We'll know more after a fuller examination."

"And what about him?"

The quick nod was toward Danny. He pried his eyes away from the rock and looked up at the doctor. A flat-faced man, he was. Nothing seemed to stand out about him, not his nose nor his mouth, and his eyes were somewhat hidden behind a pair of unobtrusive glasses Danny didn't even notice until they reflected the light. But there was nothing wrong with his voice. His voice was really sure of itself.

"He could have done it, if that's what you mean. . . . What's that on his hands?"

The woman out at Mountain View had done a lot of hollering about what was on Danny's hands, but he hadn't really noticed. He had been too busy trying to make himself believe what was going on, and then trying to make all the others not believe it. But now he could take the time to look down at his hands and see the dark stains for himself. "It's the old man's blood," Virgil said, and Danny almost fell off the chair.

"He was dead when I found him!" he yelled. "I told you already a dozen times!" But the men went right on talking, just as if he hadn't been there at all.

"I heard there was some money passed," the doctor said.

"There was," Virgil admitted. "I'm waiting now for Jim Rice to come in and make a statement."

"Well—" The doctor moved back toward the door. "I don't think I'll wait around any more. I hate leaving Miss Gaynor alone. She's taking her grandfather's death pretty hard."

"Everybody is," the deputy said.

"Just about everybody." The doctor hesitated, one hand on the doorknob, and then he came back to the sheriff's desk. "Look, Virgil," he said, "isn't there anything you can do about Trace Cooper? I picked up Joyce—Miss Gaynor—the minute I heard the news, and we went down to the mortuary to wait for the ambulance. Trace came in while we were there. You'd think he'd have some decency at a time like this!"

"I'm not Trace's keeper," Virgil growled.

"Well, he needs one! He'd been drinking again, of course, and I had to practically drive him off. Then he insisted that he wasn't there to see Joyce, that he'd come to see Francy Allen."

"Maybe he had. They were pretty friendly."

It was an awfully thin smile that touched the sheriff's lips. Danny liked him better without an expression.

"Is that anything to flaunt in Joyce's face?" Doctor Glenn demanded.

"I really wouldn't know, Lowell. This is a sheriff's office, not a court of human relations. Does Miss Gaynor want to file a complaint against Trace?"

"Why, no, I don't think so."

"Then it doesn't concern me, does it?"

Danny kind of hated to see the doctor leave. As long as he was there, the conversation didn't turn back to Danny Ross. As long as just anybody was there, he wasn't left alone with this frightening man—the sheriff. All the time he sat there, crowded on the edge of that hard oak chair, he kept telling himself this was no time to go chicken; but every now and then Virgil Keep would look at him for just a second, and Danny's argument was lost.

But he wasn't going to be alone with the man for quite a while yet. There was more phoning to do, and then more deputies and more questions. Always more questions, and always the same ones. What's your name? Danny Ross. Where are you from? Back east. Where are you going? No place. Just seeing the country. Where'd you get the money? I worked for it in a garage. Where? Back east. Where back east? It was a trap, and Danny wasn't walking into a trap. He was running away from the trap. Make it St. Louis, make it Detroit.

"Different places," he said. "I move around a lot."

"You have a home, don't you? Where's your family live?"

Danny started to sink his face into his hands, and then drew back from the terrible sight of them. If only they would let him wash the blood off his hands!

"I don't have a home!" he yelled. "I don't have a family!"

After a while he looked up and saw the tall man, Jim Rice standing beside the sheriff's desk. He couldn't remember seeing or hearing him come in, but there he was. He wasn't laughing any more.

"Well, it looks like the money I gave Doc Gaynor," he said hesitantly. "I didn't take any serial numbers or anything."

"Same denomination?"

"Hell, Virgil, I don't remember. I just peeled off some bills. Mostly twenties, I guess."

It was mostly twenties on the table. Twenties are good to carry when you're traveling. Not so bulky and not too hard to cash.

"Do you remember seeing this boy with the doctor?" Virgil asked.

There wasn't a bit of laughter about Jim Rice now. He seemed uncomfortable, but that question was easy to answer.

"Sure, he came in with Charley. The old man bought him a Coke. You know how Charley is about picking up riders on the road . . . I mean, how he was."

By this time even Danny knew how he was. He was old Charley Gaynor, the country doctor who loved everybody and was loved by everybody. Who would kill a man like that except a stranger? Who but a worthless bum mooching free rides and free drinks, and ready to kill any man for a few dollars? Danny had tried to explain about the jalopy breaking down so he wouldn't seem such a moocher, but nobody was going to swallow a yarn like that. Do you shove a car off the road because it won't run? You do if you're leaving the country and burning all your bridges behind you, but Danny couldn't tell them that.

"I can't positively identify this money," Rice added thoughtfully, "but I did pay the doctor the two hundred I owed him. If it isn't on him now, I don't know where else it could have gone."

Danny came to his feet in a hurry. "The man in the raincoat!" he yelled. "He's the one that took the money! The man in the raincoat!"

"What man?" Rice frowned. "What raincoat?"

"At the café. Sitting next to me at the counter. There was another guy in there."

How could Rice forget? The little guy with the soiled hat and the suitcase. The little guy waiting for the bus.

"I don't know," Rice said. "Maybe there was someone else at the counter. I didn't pay any attention until Charley came in, and when he left I went back to my marketing. A raincoat, you say?" The sun-dried skin began to stretch around Rice's wide mouth, and then that sharp laugh came once more. "Fine time to be wearing a raincoat," he said. "It ain't rained around here for three months!"

Darkness had drawn a blanket over Cooperton, but in some places there wouldn't be much sleep. Places like the sheriff's office, where the last deputy finally went home and Danny was left alone with the man he feared; or the

23

old frame house where Joyce Gaynor waited for a sedative—administered by an attentive young doctor—to wash away the ceiling and the pain. And over at the bar of the Pioneer Hotel, a ridiculous relic of past glory, Trace Cooper was holding a wake.

Trace was a young man with an oldish face, or maybe an old man with a youngish face—he'd forgotten which. He had red hair, red as the copper that didn't come out of the Cooper mines any more, and blue eyes and a straight nose. All of the Coopers for generations and generations had red hair, blue eyes, and straight noses, and the Coopers went right back to the Revolutionary War. Where they went before that, Trace didn't know or care. Where they were going now he did know and cared less.

"A funeral," he repeated gravely to the man behind the bar, "—we have to have a funeral for Francy. Will you come to Francy's funeral, Murph?"

Murph's head was shinier than the top surface of the bar, and it nodded like a lantern in the semidarkness. "Sure, I will, Mr. Cooper. But maybe you should get some rest now."

"No rest, Murph. No rest for the wicked."

What Murph lacked in scalp adornment he made up in eyebrows, thick and curly like little black wires, and now they were all meshed together with worry. Mr. Cooper was worse than usual tonight, much worse. It was this terrible business with Francy and now the old man, enough to upset the whole town. But the whole town wasn't at the Pioneer bar—only Trace Cooper—although from some of the talk Murph had picked up they would have been better off here.

Then Murph looked up and caught sight of a shadow coming forward out of the darkness, and he relaxed a bit. Ordinarily he couldn't have let Arthur come into the bar—not that Murph had anything against Arthur, but some folks might and you had to keep up appearances even if the Pioneer wasn't all it had once been. But Arthur was the only one in town who could manage Mr. Cooper when he got like this, so Arthur could go anywhere.

"Here's Arthur come to take you home," Murph said.

"Home?" Trace pulled his face out of the latest shot of

bourbon he'd just poured from the bottle on the bar, and peered at Murph with glassy eyes. "How's he going to do that, I wonder. I don't have a home."

"Sure you do, Mr. Cooper."

"Stop calling me Mr. Cooper!"

There was nothing puny about the fist Trace slammed down on the bar top; nothing puny about Trace at all. "I told you a dozen times—"

"Sure, Trace. Sure," Murph said.

By this time Arthur stood at Trace's shoulder like a big slice of the darkness in a white suit. Sometimes Murph wondered if Arthur wore a white suit out of defiance. You could never tell about Arthur.

"Come on, Trace, time to hit the sack," he said.

Trace turned about slowly. "Francy's dead, Arthur."

"I know. Let's go home now."

"Old Charley Gaynor's dead, too."

"That's right, old Charley Gaynor's dead. Come on—"

"Get your hands off me, you black bastard!"

Arthur had taken hold of Trace's arm, the one hanging limply at his side, but suddenly it wasn't limp any more. Suddenly it had lashed out and landed a blow across his chest, and although Arthur was a big man, he wasn't prepared for that. He fell backward, taking a couple of barstools with him, and for a moment he just sat there on his pants on the floor, and stared up at Murph. Then he got up and walked out of the bar.

"You shouldn't have said that, Mr. Cooper," Murph said. "You shouldn't have yelled at Arthur that way."

"'The good that I would I do not,'" Trace murmured, "'and the evil that I would not, that I do. . . .'" Sometimes, when the sadness came over his face, Trace Cooper looked like a poet; but the next moment he was pounding the bar again and shouting for the devil himself to hear, "Mr. Jackson! You got that, Murph? If I'm Mr. Cooper, then Arthur's Mr. Jackson!"

"Sure, Mr. Cooper. Sure."

With Arthur gone it was going to be a rough night; now Murph was really getting worried. It wasn't as if Trace Cooper was a bum to be thrown out on his ear. Trace was— well he was a Cooper, and this was Cooperton. Maybe it wasn't much of a town and maybe Trace wasn't much of a Cooper, but you had to keep up appearances. Besides, Murph liked Trace. Crazy as hell, he was, and always had been, but he couldn't help liking him—except for the times he hated his guts. Like now, for instance, when he wanted to close up and call it a day. There was no trade tonight with the town at the edge of its nerves.

But just as he was thinking this, another customer came into the bar, and the sight of this particular customer made Murph's big Irish mouth drop wide open. At first he thought he was seeing things, but no, not another man in these parts could approach a bar like an ambassador entering an official reception, and not another man wore English-made suits with a folded handkerchief nosing up from the breast pocket.

"Yes, sir," Murph said, squaring his shoulders, "what'll you have, Mr. Laurent?"

That brought Trace away from the bourbon bottle. He turned around with his back against the bar and attempted a bow that, fortunately, didn't end in disaster. "Senator Laurent!" he said.

"Thank you," Laurent murmured. "I'm not a senator, but I appreciate the honor."

"You wouldn't if you knew what I think of senators! But you look the way a senator should look. Doesn't he look like a senator, Murph?"

Murph was a little flustered. In the five years Alexander Laurent had been living in these parts this was the second time he'd set foot in the Pioneer Hotel. The first time was the day he'd come to see Trace Cooper about the sale of the old Cooper ranch. And who was this Laurent? Not being up on such matters, Murph wasn't sure—but it was something important, famous even. A lawyer, that was it. A famous trial lawyer, but now he was retired and standing before Murph's bar instead of a bar of justice. Murph began to chuckle at his own joke, which couldn't be appreciated since he'd kept it to himself. To cover his embarrassment, he repeated the standard greeting to all new faces before him.

"What'll you have?"

Laurent considered the matter with grave eyes. He

looked about him, picked out a booth at the far side of the room, and said:

"Whatever Mr. Cooper is having—and in a booth, please. Will you join me, Mr. Cooper?"

"Sorry," Trace said, "I'm busy. I'm arranging a funeral."

"Isn't this a peculiar place for doing that?"

"That's what I've been telling him," Murph broke in, but Trace silenced him with one defiant glance. "Not at all!" he insisted. "I spoke to the good Reverend Whitlow this afternoon, but he didn't seem very happy about putting in a word for a sinner. I don't think he could anyway. If I know Francy she won't even show up at the pearly gates; she'll go around to the family entrance." Trace finished off the rest of his drink and smiled crookedly at the empty glass. "But you didn't know Francy," he reflected. "Only the worst people knew Francy. She was a cute kid, wasn't she, Murph?"

"She wasn't exactly a kid any more," Murph said.

"Nor am I," Laurent observed ruefully. "At my age a barstool can become extremely uncomfortable. Bartender—"

By the simple means of snatching Trace's bottle from under his nose, Laurent achieved the impossible: he took Trace away from the bar. Of course he took him only as far as a booth across the floor, but even that was progress. Murph followed with a pair of glasses, and then returned to the business of preparing to close up. Maybe the great Alexander Laurent could do something with Trace.

The first thing Laurent did was to remove his expensive straw hat and place it on the seat beside him. The light from an ornate wall bracket, long since converted to electricity, danced over the deep waves of his silver hair, and his steady gray eyes studied Trace Cooper's face for several moments before he spoke.

"I understand that you are an attorney, Mr. Cooper," he said at last.

"Who told you that?" Trace countered.

"One of the few friends I had—Doctor Gaynor."

The name had a sobering effect. The drink Trace had poured himself just sat there for a while. "I knew the old man went out to the ranch now and then," he said, "but I didn't know you had such dull conversations."

"Oh, they weren't dull, Mr. Cooper. The doctor told me a great deal about this town and its inhabitants. I was particularly interested in the Coopers, of course."

"Why, is the house haunted?"

"The house is charming."

"And comfortable, Mr. Laurent? Roomy, spacious—"

"All of those things. Your forebears built well."

"But on the sand," Trace muttered. "What's this talk all about anyway? Surely you don't need a lawyer!"

The remark was supposed to be funny, but Laurent didn't copy Trace's twisted smile. Instead he grew even more grave. "Someone needs a lawyer," he said. "You must know what happened at Mountain View today. Old Dr. Gaynor was murdered and robbed of a sum of money he had just received on the premises. The sheriff is holding a young hitchhiker the doctor picked up on the road."

Laurent spoke quietly but the magic of a voice that had held juries spellbound was not lost. Trace had to listen.

"Virgil Keep is no fool. He's holding the boy incommunicado until his case is airtight, but you can't keep secrets in this town. Already there are troubling rumors. If this Danny Ross is guilty of murder he deserves a fair trial; but if he is innocent—" Laurent paused to give his argument the needed force. "If he is innocent, Mr. Cooper, then the murderer of my friend goes free."

It wasn't easy for Trace to follow Laurent's words, and all that bourbon he'd consumed didn't help a bit. And yet the very tone of his voice was saying that this was important, this he must understand.

"Make your point," Trace said.

Laurent smiled faintly. "To ascertain the facts in a murder case requires a great deal of investigation. There are reasons, personal reasons, why I can't do the job myself. That's why I've come to you."

"To me!" Trace had tried hard to take this conversation seriously, but now he threw back his head and laughed. "The great Alexander Laurent," he cried, "comes to me!"

"The old, weary Alexander Laurent," answered the man across the table, "asks you to help him—and Danny Ross."

■   ■   ■

28

Danny was crying. The one thing he'd promised himself he wouldn't do, no matter what, and the first blow had set him bawling like a baby. "Get up!" Virgil said, and Danny couldn't do anything else with that big hand on his collar. He knew what he was supposed to say, but the words wouldn't come. They wouldn't have done any good anyway, because all that anger in the big man's eyes hadn't been put there by a skinny kid in levis. Now Danny was on his feet again, propped up against the wall of the cell and tensed for the next blow.

"Virgil! Virgil, what are you doing?"

Danny wished the woman would stay out of it—she only made the sheriff angrier; but Ada was at the cell door, her eyes wide and moist, and her rough hands grasping the bars.

"Get the hell back where you belong!" Virgil roared.

"He's only a boy, Virgil!"

"A boy? He's old enough, Ada, even for you. He wears pants—"

The second blow was more vicious than the first. Danny crumpled like an empty sack and slid halfway down the wall before that heavy hand grabbed his collar again. For a minute he thought his head was splitting, on account of the ringing, and then the ringing became the phone on the sheriff's desk in the next room. Virgil, straddle-legged and tall, turned his head. Oh, God, keep it ringing!

Through a corridor of pain and distance Danny heard the woman's trembling voice.

"Yes, this is the sheriff's office. Yes, Virgil's here. The Pioneer Hotel? Yes, Mr. Murphy, I'll tell him to hurry."

Yes, please tell him to hurry. Hurry someplace—any place out of this cell! Danny raised his head and saw Ada back at the bars again talking rapidly, mentioning a name he'd heard before. Trace Cooper. Trace Cooper was drunk and tearing up somebody's bar. The sheriff muttered an oath and let loose of Danny's collar. God bless, Danny breathed, God bless a drunk—Trace Cooper.

Chapter Four

There's never been a night yet that didn't end eventually. Danny's ended with a metallic crash, a heavy thud, and a man's brief curse. At first Danny thought it was just a continuation of the bad dreams he'd been having, but then he opened his eyes and blinked at the early morning sunlight streaming over the high window sill. Just the sunlight, way out there in the open beyond the bars, but it was a wonderful thing to know the night was over at last. While he was trying to remember where he was, and why the dreams had been so frightening, reality moved in and began to take over where the dreams left off.

The bars were real. The hardness under him was a narrow cot, and every muscle in his body protested when Danny shifted his weight and propped himself up on one elbow. He was locked in a small cell—a cage actually, separated from a similar cell by a partition of bars. In this adjoining cell a man with red hair was sitting on the floor trying to pry one foot out of a tin bucket.

"Worst damn hotel in town," the man muttered. "Sometimes I wonder why I keep coming back."

Now Danny began to remember about the man in the next cell. Quite a scrapper he was. The sheriff was no midget by any means, but he'd had his hands full putting this boy away. In the effort he seemed to forget all about Danny Ross and the confession he was supposed to make, and that alone was reason enough to make this man a friend. The crooked grin on his face was another.

"At least when I fell out of bed I landed on my—on the bucket," Trace Cooper said. "You must have landed on your face."

Danny caught on to what the man was talking about when he tried to open his mouth. There was a cut on his lower lip that gave his mouth that rusty iron taste, and his jaw was swollen until it seemed out of line. But Danny had enough trouble without asking for more. He leaned back on the cot again and closed his eyes.

"Antisocial," Trace muttered. "It's not bad enough that he kills old man Gaynor, he has to be unfriendly besides."

"I didn't kill the old man!" Danny yelled. "I didn't kill anybody!"

Danny's head almost flew off when he jumped up from the cot so fast. He stumbled and grabbed hold of the bars for support. His legs were like old rubber bands.

"Take it easy," Trace said. "I don't care if you did kill him. He lived long enough—maybe too long."

"That's a crazy thing to say!"

"Why? Three score and ten, that's all the Bible gives you. Charley had a couple of years on the good book at that."

There was no way to figure this character. He had kicked away the bucket but was still sitting on the floor, cross-legged and relaxed, as if he owned the place. Aside from an overnight growth of rusty beard and the slept-in condition of his suit, he seemed no worse for the load he'd carried in with him. He hauled a pack of cigarettes and a folder of matches from one wrinkled jacket pocket and lit up, then stuck the matches inside the pack and tossed them to Danny.

"Thanks," Danny said. "The sheriff took mine last night."

"When he took the money," Trace suggested.

"It's my money! I worked for that dough!"

"How much did the old man have, anyway? There's a story going around that it was three—four hundred dollars."

"Two hundred," Danny said.

"Then you did take it."

"The hell I did! I saved six months to get that bank roll. It was that guy in the raincoat—"

But Danny didn't get a chance to go into that story again just then; somebody was approaching down the hall, and maybe it was just as well not to be caught talking to the other prisoner. It didn't take much to irritate the sheriff. But it wasn't Virgil Keep who came to the door of Trace Cooper's cell. It was Ada, her faded hair in curlers and her meager figure encased in a loose-fitting robe. She was bearing a tray of food that smelled strongly of hot coffee.

"I thought I heard you awake in here," she said brightly. "How are you feeling this morning, Mr. Cooper?"

Nice and friendly, Danny thought. Even extra friendly, as if this redhead was a distinguished guest instead of an overnight lockup. And get that *Mister* Cooper! . . . only the way Ada pronounced it made the name sound like Cupper.

The man on the floor struggled to his feet and executed a mock bow. "All things considered, not too bad," he answered.

"I wondered after last night."

"Was it worse than usual last night?"

"Much worse, Mr. Cooper. But then I guess you were feeling bad about Francy and poor Dr. Gaynor."

A shadow crossed Trace's face, dark but swift. Then he brightened. "Here, let me take the tray, Ada. Don't tell me it's oatmeal again!"

"I'm afraid so, the county—"

"I know, I know. The county allows only fifty cents a day for feeding prisoners. Here, give mine to my friend in the other cell. He looks as though he needs something strengthening."

Suddenly Danny was starving hungry. Last night he couldn't have swallowed a bite even if the sheriff had allowed Ada to feed him, which he wouldn't; but murder or no murder, phony charge or no phony charge, Danny was young with an appetite to match. There was oatmeal and coffee and a couple of pieces of wilted toast on the tray, but it might have been top sirloin from the way Danny dug in.

"Ada, my love," Trace said through the bars, "did I ever tell you that your coffee tastes like liquefied charcoal?"

"You mustn't talk that way," she protested. "Virgil might hear."

"If he hasn't found out by this time, he'll never know," Trace muttered, but Danny could see that the woman wasn't joking. She looked frightened, almost as if Cooper had made a pass at her—and that was about the silliest thing imaginable. But then again maybe it wasn't, because now the sheriff had stepped into the hall with the wrath of Jehovah on his dour morning face.

"Ada, what are you doing out here?" he demanded. "Get back to the kitchen!"

"I was just bringing breakfast to the prisoners," she stammered.

"In your nightgown? Couldn't you put some clothes on before parading around, or would that spoil your fun?"

Ada reached up instinctively and pulled the collar of her robe tighter about her stringy throat. If she was wearing a nightgown under that garment it certainly couldn't be seen, for the skirt swept the top of her scuffed houseslippers. What could be seen were the quick tears that brightened her eyes as she backed off down the hall, and something else too. Something almost like a smile. How that could be Danny didn't know, but in a world so full of strange and terrible things anything was possible.

But Virgil wasn't smiling. He had the briefest of glances for Danny, and a few choice words for Trace Cooper. "It beats me why you do it," he said. "Why can't you leave that poison alone?"

"Every man to his own poison," Trace murmured. "I don't bother you about yours."

"Mine? I don't know what you're talking about. I never touch the stuff. . . . What the devil's going to become of you, Trace? You're not a rich man any more."

"I don't need you to tell me that, Virgil."

"Then straighten up and stop acting like a kid! For a while after you came home I actually thought the Army had made a man of you—"

"The Army!" Trace grinned and threw Danny a broad wink. "What's so wonderful about the Army? It's just a lot of civilians wearing the same kind of pants."

Maybe it wasn't the funniest crack in the world, but Danny laughed, high-pitched and nervous like the way he felt every time the sheriff looked at him. And the laugh was a big mistake because it set him up right in the center of attention. It gave Virgil an easy way out of a losing argument.

"Well, look who's feeling so chipper!" he said, and Danny wilted.

"He doesn't look chipper to me," Trace remarked. "Funny thing, Virgil, but I never knew before that cells have doorknobs."

"You keep out of this!"

"Why? I'm a taxpayer."

"So was old Charley Gaynor, but he's not any more."

"I told you last night, I told you a hundred times," Danny protested, "I never killed the old man! I never even touched his wallet!"

All this time Trace had been participating in the conversation with a sort of sleepy-eyed indifference, but now he became interested. A wallet? What wallet? What did Virgil have on the kid anyway? Virgil was too astonished at the thought of anybody in Cooperton not knowing all about Danny Ross to be exclusive. He spelled out the whole story, right from the moment Danny had walked into Walter Wade's café with the doctor until he'd been discovered standing beside the corpse with bloodstained hands and a pocket full of money.

"But what about the wallet?" Trace insisted. "If the kid took it shouldn't it be on him?"

Virgil snorted. "Of course not! Why would he keep incriminating evidence like that. He had plenty of time to throw the wallet away before Viola and Walter found him."

"Then it's still out there somewhere. Why don't we look for it?"

Virgil's head might look like a chopping block, but it wasn't that thick. A scouting expedition to Mountain View was the first item on his morning agenda, and he would have explained that to Trace in no uncertain terms except for one word in the redhead's question. "We?" Virgil echoed.

"Sure," Trace said, "you and Danny and me. You because you need that wallet for evidence, Danny because he knows where he threw it, and me because—" Trace stretched out his long arms and yawned. "—because Murph will never prefer charges for what I did to his bar, and there's nothing like a ride in the country to clear a morning-after head."

Trace Cooper seemed to get everything he wanted. Everything he asked for, everything he said—that's how it happened.

"Call Arthur and have him pick me up in the jeep," he ordered, and the sheriff, like an obedient servant, trotted to comply. Everybody hopped when Cooper spoke, maybe because he expected them to hop. Danny would have to watch this and see how it was done.

It was still early when they left town. The stores along Main Street weren't open yet, and the attendants at a couple of gas stations passed on the way were just getting the pumps unlocked. Danny wasn't alone with the sheriff on this ride. Not one, but two, deputies were included in the expedition, and right behind the sheriff's sedan rolled a bright red jeep driven by a big black in an Army issue windbreaker with Trace Cooper lounging on the seat beside him.

"Why the escort?" the younger deputy asked. "What's Trace got on his mind?"

The sheriff shrugged. "What mind?" he challenged.

But it was a beautiful morning, still cool enough for Danny's leather jacket although the sun was getting warmer with each degree it mounted. Over the mountains lining both sides of the road a veil of mist stretched thinner and thinner until it pulled apart and began to disappear before his eyes, and there were bird songs and pungent mustard smells that made the earth seem good again, and made death a faraway thing that wasn't going to happen until he was too old to care. This time yesterday Danny was driving the old jalopy toward a dot on the map called Red Rock; this time tomorrow he should have been safely across the border. Those things were real and rational; only the present was a lie.

Even that cluster of faded yellow buildings at the crossroads looked pleasant in the morning sunlight until the sight of a tired old sedan brought back a bloody memory. Virgil pulled off the road and parked alongside the deserted vehicle. The hood was down now and no visible remnant of violence remained, but Danny's dread needed no stimulant. The beauty of the morning was lost.

The little red jeep bounced across the gravel and stopped just short of the yellow building.

"Well, here we are," Trace called cheerfully, hopping down from the front seat. "Now let's re-enact the crime."

"If you don't mind," Virgil muttered, "I'm in charge here."

"Of course you are, but isn't that how it's done? Just where was the doctor when you found him?"

Danny shivered, and it wasn't that cool, but there was no way out of it. He had to go over the whole thing again, pacing out his movements, pointing out where the old man hung over the radiator, where the bloody rock had lain, where he was when he heard the car driving away. "The bus made so much noise pulling away that I couldn't be sure about the car. But if it didn't come from here, where did it come from?"

By this time Walter Wade had joined the party, a ragged sweater encasing his narrow shoulders and the soft morning wind ruffling the few fine strands of hair still remaining on his head.

"Maybe it was Jim Rice leaving," Walter suggested.

"What kind of car does he drive?" Danny asked.

"Do you mean you can tell what kind of car you heard?"

"No, but I could tell what kind I didn't hear. This was a smooth-running job with a fast pickup. It had to be to leave without being noticed, bus or no bus."

"Providing there was a car," Virgil muttered.

"Jim has a new, well, almost new pickup," Walter said, "but I think he pulled out before the bus did. Leastways, he left before you did."

"Sure, and so did the guy in the raincoat. You remember the guy in the raincoat, don't you?"

Walter hesitated. After all, this talk was a little silly. Why, with his own eyes he'd seen this boy— But Walter wasn't as self-assured as his wife, and there had been a man in a raincoat.

"You mean the passenger for the bus?" he asked. "I guess that was a raincoat he was wearing."

"There, you see? I told you!"

Danny had no reason to sound so happy. The man in the raincoat was a long way off by this time, and if he had killed the old man, he sure wasn't coming back to confess. But it seemed good to prove any part of his story; any part was better than none. And then Trace Cooper came ambling up from where he'd been examining the gravel drive behind the shed. "What's this about a man in a raincoat?" he asked. "Seems I heard him mentioned earlier this morning."

So Danny went through the story again: the man in the raincoat sitting next to him at the counter, watching the doctor take that money from Jim Rice, and going out a few minutes after the old man left. "He asked for the men's room," Danny recalled, and all eyes turned back toward the long, yellow building. Two thirds of the way back from the front corner was a door lettered "Men," not thirty feet away from the doctor's old sedan. Trace was the first to speak.

"How long was he gone?" he asked.

"I don't know exactly," Danny admitted. "He put a coin in the juke box and then said he didn't like the music. The record finished playing, and I sat there a few minutes longer, maybe five altogether. This guy Rice went out, like Walter says, and then I went out. The bus was pulling up then."

"And did the man in the raincoat get on the bus?"

"He must have. He was running for it when I started around to the doc's car. . . . Hell, I told all this to the sheriff last night!"

Telling the story to Trace Cooper was a lot different from telling it to the sheriff; Trace listened. He listened with his ears, with his eyes, and with the fists knotted inside his pants pockets. He wasn't quite so tall a man as he'd seemed in the cell, but the sunlight made a torch of his bright hair, and to Danny Ross he suddenly became a guardian angel with a halo of fire on his head.

"Don't you think you'd better check on this man, Virgil?" he said.

"I came out here to look for a wallet," Virgil said.

"Let your deputies look for it. Who was this fellow, Walter?"

"Search me," Walter shrugged. "Somebody from the mine crew I suppose. I never saw him before."

"Where was he going?"

"You'll have to ask Viola. She talked to him, not me."

Trace considered the matter for all of thirty seconds and then clapped Danny on the shoulder with one steady hand. "Come on, kid," he said, "let's see what kind of coffee they serve in this café. That place we had breakfast was strictly a dump!"

Chapter Five

Danny had an ally. He didn't know why Trace Cooper was on his side; maybe he was just one of those guys who had to say no because everybody else was saying yes, but something happened inside the Mountain View café that gave him a sort of left-handed clue. It was after he'd shown Trace and the sheriff where he had sat at the counter, and where the man in the raincoat sat. It was after Viola's surly answers that didn't tell a thing about the stranger except that he'd come down from the mine. (Viola knew a killer when she saw one—what was the use of all this talk?) It was during the coffee and doughnuts, while the sheriff was making a phone call, that a car drove up to the pumps outside and two people came in. One Danny recognized: he was the young doctor who had visited the sheriff's office last night. The other was a girl.

One look at the girl and Trace stopped eating; one look at Trace and the girl turned pale. She was a pretty girl, too. Old, of course—twenty-five maybe—but with a good figure and a nice, full mouth. Her sun-bleached hair was tied back with a little black ribbon, schoolgirl fashion, but it was her eyes that had time and trouble in them. Danny understood when he realized who she was. Her name was Joyce Gaynor, and her grandfather was laid out on a slab at the mortuary.

"Oh," was all the sound she made at the sight of Trace. He came to his feet, but before he could speak Dr. Glenn came between them.

"Are you following Miss Gaynor?" Glenn demanded.

It was a pretty silly question, seeing that Trace had come in first—a small matter he was quick to point out.

"And it never occurred to you that Miss Gaynor would be out to pick up her grandfather's car!"

"Frankly, no," Trace admitted, "but it does occur to me that she's not going to get it without the sheriff's permission. You can take that up with him yourself. I'm just having a cup of coffee."

"Well, at least you've changed your diet!" Glenn muttered.

Danny didn't know what this feud was all about, but wherever a female was involved he could use his imagination. Joyce Gaynor had only moved a few steps inside the door, and so far she hadn't noticed Danny at all. She was staring at Trace, and he was staring back. They were having quite a conversation without words when the sheriff returned and broke it up.

"Well, I got the guy's name," he said. "Malone. Steve Malone. He quit Raney yesterday."

Trace managed to pry his eyes away from the girl. "Quit?" he echoed.

"Quit or was fired. Raney's out with the road crew and I talked with some punk who didn't know much except that Malone pulled out yesterday. Must be the same fellow. He was the only one who left camp."

"For where?"

Virgil shrugged his heavy shoulders. "You name it. Maybe Raney knows; I don't."

Doctor Glenn's eyes were shining bright blue behind his glasses. "Who is Malone?" he demanded.

"The man in the raincoat," Virgil answered.

They were going to leave it like that. Danny began to feel panicky again just when he'd started feeling good; but then Trace spoke up. "It can't be over twenty miles to Raney's mine," he suggested.

"Are you suggesting that I drive up there?" Virgil asked.

"Why not? The county pays for the gas."

"If you ask me, it's a wild-goose chase!"

"Who is the man in the raincoat?" the young doctor pleaded, and Trace grinned at him. "Malone," he said. "Steve Malone. . . . Shall we get started, Virgil?"

So they weren't going to leave it at that after all. Danny began to relax again—he even helped himself to another doughnut—but Viola, who had been watching him like a hawk all this time, had to start yelling and throwing a shoe. "If you're going up to that mine you take this murderer with you!" she shouted at the sheriff. "I don't want him hanging around my place!"

"Murderer?"

It wasn't a nice word to throw around in any company, but that girl in the doorway wasn't exactly neutral. She moved forward quickly, her eyes round and terrible. "Is this the one?" she demanded. "Is this the hitchhiker?"

"This is Danny Ross," Trace said. "He rode in with your grandfather."

"And killed him!"

"Nobody knows that, Joyce. It's just supposition."

"I know!" Viola began, but the words were barely out when Trace's casual manner vanished in a flood of anger. "You know nothing!" he snapped. "You know only what you want to know and unless it's bad enough, unless it tears somebody to pieces, you're stone deaf! That seems to be a common ailment around here, but I'm stuck with the old-fashioned idea that the accused is innocent until proven guilty . . . any accused."

The words may have been for Viola, but Trace's eyes were only for the girl. "Come, Joyce," the young doctor said, "Let's get out of here."

"That's right, Joyce, listen to the doctor. It saves thinking for yourself."

"Now just a minute, Cooper—"

"I don't have a minute," Trace said. "I have no more time for you than you had for Francy lying out there on the road. It's too bad old Charley didn't keep such strict office hours; she could have died in the dirt where she belonged."

It was the slamming door that ended this exchange, but not before Dr. Glenn's final shot. "At least," he said, with a glare for Danny, "your choice of companions is consistent."

That was Danny's clue, and he mulled it over all the way to the mine. People were a lot like motors: the bugs always showed up in performance, and from what Danny had seen of this neighborhood it had plenty of bugs. Even the dead man, old Dr. Gaynor, had been a queer one, and that was a whole nest of crackpots he had walked in on at Mountain View. Viola had a one-track mind, exactly one track more than her husband, and Jim Rice, with that ready laugh of his, would probably be convulsed by a public hanging. As for Ada Keep, there was an item for anybody's family album! Danny shuddered. There was only one person here he could understand and anticipate, and that one filled him with terror. He glanced at the rear-view mirror and felt better at the sight of the little red jeep following behind them. For some reason the sheriff wasn't so frightening with Trace Cooper around.

Twenty miles can be quick or twenty miles can be painful; on this road they were both. The road began to spiral upward a few miles east of Mountain View, but Virgil drove without regard for bumps, dips, or sudden curves. He drove like a man who knows what lies ahead and is grimly determined to get it over with, devil take the chuckholes. Now the valley slipped away below them, and that low swell of mountains became a wall of ragged boulders towering overhead. Danny had no idea what they might be mining up yonder, but it must be diamonds to be worth the climb.

Then suddenly the road widened and flattened out, and a cluster of tents and sheds appeared on a clearing up ahead. Virgil slackened speed and braked to a quick stop alongside a passing laborer. "Raney around?" he called. His answer was a nod and a thumb jerked toward one of the tents.

It was a lonely place they had come to. Danny remembered the way Steve Malone had paced before that juke box, and began to understand his anxiety to get away. A worker's camp on a mountainside would have been hell for a man like Malone, but Danny kind of liked it. These mountains now, couldn't a man get lost in them? Couldn't he escape the world of clocks and crisis and learn to live again? Who needed civilization anyway? It was a lovely thought, but that gun on Virgil's hip was no toy, and they hadn't come so far just to admire the scenery.

"Enjoy the ride?" Trace called, as the jeep skidded to a stop beside the sheriff's sedan. Danny grinned weakly. He already had a premonition of futility, and when the man Raney appeared (tall, of course, with bony features and faraway eyes), he didn't have long to wait for confirmation.

"Malone? Sure, I had a man named Malone working for me, but not any more. He went down the hill yesterday. . . . No, I don't know where you might find him. He was no miner, just a bum I picked up in Junction City a couple of weeks ago."

"A couple of weeks?" Trace echoed. "He must not have drawn much pay."

41

"They never do. I get 'em like that all the time, dead broke and crying for a job—any kind of a job. Two or three weeks and their throats get dry and their feet start itching. That's the last I see of 'em." Raney paused and spat hard against the yellow dust at his feet. "What's the trouble, sheriff? What's Malone done?"

"Nothing," Virgil said quickly, "nothing important. I just thought he might have been witness to something that happened down at Mountain View yesterday."

"The old doctor?" Raney's interest perked up immediately. "I heard about that. Heard you got the killer, too. Some punk kid . . ." Danny had remained inside the sedan, but he could hear the conversation through the open window. It was enough to make him slump down in the seat. ". . . Sorry I can't help you, sheriff," Raney concluded, "but men like Malone just don't leave forwarding addresses. He might have been heading for the coast. I heard him talking one day about all the easy money he could make just putting in time at some aircraft plant."

So the sheriff was right after all, and it was just a wild-goose chase. Losing heart this way was even worse than what had happened to Danny the day before, because then the world crashed so suddenly that he at least had the anesthesia of shock to make it bearable. Now there was nothing—no hope and no way out. Malone was on his way to the coast, and a fat chance the sheriff was going to look for him! Even if he did, even if Malone was found, was he likely to have that two hundred dollars? Was he likely to confess just to save Danny Ross?

It was the same road going down the mountain as going up, but now it rolled too easily underneath the wheels; now it wasn't long enough. The red jeep was still bouncing along behind, but not for long. A few miles short of the Mountain View crossing it turned south on one of the little one-track trails that laced the valley, and as it disappeared from the rear-view mirror Danny's panic returned. Even Trace Cooper had deserted him now. From here on it was just Danny looking out for himself.

42

Chapter Six

To anyone knowing this country all the little one-track trails led somewhere, and Trace knew it like no other man. This particular trail he knew better than all the rest even though he had been avoiding it for almost five years. It was in better shape now, graded and graveled the way it would be for a man wealthy enough to keep up the old Cooper ranch. And it was still called the Cooper ranch and always would be. Laurent was a foreigner. Laurent was a man from the land of smoke and steel where the mountains have windows and self-service elevators; but the Coopers had come in covered wagons—and passed in covered coffins. The Coopers belonged.

The last of the Coopers, being a man of impulse, hadn't given Arthur much warning of his decision. "Turn left," he ordered, and Arthur turned left. They were a strange pair, this big Negro and the man with the flaming red hair, and it had given Cooperton a lot to talk about when Trace came back from the war with his new companion. That was just dandy with Trace. The more they talked, the better he liked it. But Arthur Jackson wasn't a whim; he was a partner. He was an inspiration! The idea had hit Trace while he was overseas: the longing hunger to return to the soil and become the solid citizen he'd never been. But how? All Trace knew was the art of spending other people's money and drinking anybody's liquor. But there in his own company was a man who had learned long ago that he must fight for every inch of the way. It seemed a happy combination.

All of this ancient history passed through Trace's mind on the road to the ranch house. They'd made a stab at it that first year, a real try; but the land is like a woman—neglect her too long and she belongs to someone else. The sale to Laurent had just covered the debts and the price of a few acres at the edge of town.

"The place looks good," Trace said.

Arthur gave the accelerator an extra kick. "Forget about

43

the place," he muttered. "You've got a nice place of your own."

But it did look good. The house was tucked deep within the valley where a crooked river, almost dry this late in the summer, snaked its way through an oasis of scrub foliage. At a time when architectural fashion dictated cupolas and laced balustrades, the Coopers had built low to the ground—rambling and heavy-beamed with thick walls to insulate against the sun. A flash of pink and scarlet marked the flower beds, and from his ease on the broad patio a tall man with silver hair watched the jeep race into the courtyard and stop in a cloud of dust.

"Good morning, Mr. Cooper," he said, as Trace leaped to the ground. "I've been expecting you."

Alexander Laurent was immaculately attired in a pale blue tropical worsted suit that made the blue of his eyes deep as an evening sky. The inevitable handkerchief peeked from his breast pocket, and a pastel tie was as carefully knotted as if he were on his way to court. He didn't rise, but beckoned Trace to join him in one of the padded chairs grouped about a wrought-iron and glass table already laid for two.

"We were just about to have lunch," he explained. "Ramón, set another place for Mr. Cooper."

The patio was shaded and cool. Trace glanced back to where Arthur waited in the sun drenched jeep and then stopped the dark-skinned servant with a gesture of his hand. "No, thanks," he said. "I can't stay. I just dropped by to see if I heard you correctly last night. I was quite drunk at the time."

"You heard correctly." Laurent smiled.

"Then you're really serious about taking this case?"

"I am serious about you taking it, Mr. Cooper. I shall, of course, offer every possible assistance."

"Why?"

The question was out before Trace could hold his tongue. "I told you last night," Laurent answered. "I wish to know the truth about this horrible crime. Dr. Gaynor was my friend."

"Dr. Gaynor was everybody's friend, but I wouldn't say he was yours in particular."

From inside the house came the sound of music, a piano being played with the sensitive fingers of a master. Laurent raised his head and gazed across the valley. The noonday heat shimmered like a silver curtain between the ranch and the mountains, and no wind stirred.

"Let's put it another way then," he said. "Let's say that life gets dull without challenge. Danny Ross is a challenge. Is he guilty, or is he innocent? The mob says guilty, and so I must say innocent. That's the story of my life, Mr. Cooper. Does it answer your question?"

"One of them," Trace admitted, "but it only makes the other more difficult. What I've been wondering for the past five years is why a man retires at the peak of his career. Why he leaves the world he's brought to heel and buries himself—"

"—in this beautiful, peaceful valley," Laurent finished. "I'm an old man, Mr. Cooper."

"Sixty-one. Fifty-six when you quit your practice."

"You seem to know a great deal about me."

Trace pulled up just in time. Every man has to believe in something, and a much younger Trace Cooper had believed in Alexander Laurent and followed his career like some bobby-soxer with a fan magazine. As foolish, too. The Coopers were practical people; when they studied law it was to use it for their own advantage.

"I went to law school," he reminded. "Any law student knows a great deal about Alexander Laurent."

"And now we are working together. I'm flattered, Mr. Cooper, but please tell me what you've learned. I doubt that you came here for the ride."

Trace leaned back and relaxed. Never mind the personal equations; the problem was Danny Ross. "You aroused my curiosity last night," he began. "After you left, I heaved a bottle at the mirror over the bar. Ross couldn't be incommunicado with me installed in the adjoining cell."

"Ingenious," Laurent murmured.

"Not at all. I've broken about six of those mirrors already; the result is always the same. This morning I had a talk with Danny."

"Did you come to any conclusions?"

"I never come to conclusions—that's the story of my life— but I did learn one thing that seems important: Danny doesn't have Charley Gaynor's wallet. He has two hundred dollars he insists are his, but the wallet is missing. The sheriff thinks Danny threw it away and has a couple of men searching the grounds at Mountain View right now."

The music from inside the house was getting louder. Trace had to raise his voice to go on.

"I don't think they're going to find it. I watched Danny when the search was getting started. If anyone had come close, come anywhere near where he'd thrown the thing, he would have shown some anxiety. The kid's just too scared to put up a front."

"Then I take it that he betrayed no unusual emotion."

"That's right. He just kept insisting the wallet was lifted by a man in the café who was waiting for the bus to Junction City."

Like Danny Ross, Laurent had betrayed no unusual emotion up to this point. Now he leaned forward, tense and alert. "And was there such a man?" he asked.

"There was," Trace said. "A man named Steve Malone."

He had to relate the whole story then: Danny's version of Malone's behavior in the café, the way he'd met him running for the bus, and finally the discouraging results of that trip to the mine. It was the tale of a rolling stone, a little man in a raincoat whose destination was always unknown but might be the west coast. "That covers a lot of territory," he conceded, "but the sheriff will get out a 'man wanted' on him. He may not want to, but it's his duty and Virgil's a stickler for duty. Of course, that may take time."

"During which Malone could easily spend the evidence," Laurent added.

"But he would still have the doctor's wallet."

"Possibly." Laurent leaned back in his chair again, but his eyes were busy. "Then I assume you intend to sit tight until the sheriff brings in Malone," he said. "An easy way, Mr. Cooper, but hardly practical. Suppose the man is found and questioned. What's to stop him from turning state's evidence against Danny Ross in order to save his own skin? After all, there's a great deal of difference between the penalty for theft and the penalty for murder. No, I'm afraid Malone isn't going to be very helpful to Danny unless we find him first."

It was Trace's turn to crowd the edge of his chair now. "But how?" he demanded, and Laurent smiled. "Imagination, Mr. Cooper, imagination," he said. "As you were telling me about Malone just now I received the distinct impression that I'd come across his type before . . . restless, unreliable, fond of easy money and a good time. Now let's assume that Danny Ross is innocent and that our Mr. Malone did kill the doctor and take his wallet. What did he do then?"

"Caught the bus for Junction City," Trace said.

"And when would that bus have reached its destination?"

"About six thirty."

"At the end of the day," Laurent mused, "and our Mr. Malone had been living in a camp on the side of a mountain for several weeks. Now he has money in his pockets; now he's not on that mountainside. I put it to you, Mr. Cooper, do you really think it likely that he boarded the first bus going west?"

"He was running away," Trace reminded.

"But it's so easy to find a man when he's running. He boards a bus and there he is, all locked in and ready for that policeman waiting at the end of the line. But if he holes in somewhere—"

It was the crash of battered notes from the piano that broke into Laurent's conjecture. He smiled and nodded to the silent servant nearby. "You may start serving now, Ramón," he directed. "It seems that Douglas has concluded his practicing. I don't believe you have met my son, Mr. Cooper. . . ."

At first Trace thought it was a boy who came through the doorway onto the patio. He was slender, lithe, and casually dressed in white slacks and a knitted sport shirt. Just a boy, fair and delicately handsome; but as he came closer the years crept into his face until they were gathered almost forty in number. Douglas Laurent, the only child of an illustrious father.

"Come sit down, Douglas," Laurent urged. "This is Mr. Cooper, the gentleman from whom I purchased the ranch."

"It's hot," Douglas said, with a brief nod toward Trace. "I simply can't work when it's hot."

"Douglas is writing a concerto," the elder Laurent explained. "It's quite an undertaking."

47

"It's impossible!" Douglas snapped. "This weather, this country, this house!"

"What's wrong with the house?" Trace demanded.

"It's cavernous! The acoustics are terrible! This time of year back home—" Douglas's face grew radiant with remembrance, "—this time of year we would go to the lake house. It was small and quiet, and I had a little studio of my own over the barn. But what's the use of talking about it? Father likes it here."

"I used to have a cabin—you might call it a cottage—at the rim of Peace Canyon," Trace recalled. "It might make a fair studio."

"Peace Canyon? Is that what you call it?"

"Then you know the place?"

Expressions chased across Douglas's handsome face like clouds and sunlight playing tag in a troubled sky. Now he was gay, now grave. "I know the place," he murmured. "It's horrible!"

"Douglas—"

Laurent must have gauged the irritation mounting in Trace's reddening face. His voice was like a whip, and then it became a caress. "Ramón is waiting to serve the salad," he said. "Can't we change your mind about lunch, Mr. Cooper?"

"I'm afraid not," Trace said. "It's over a hundred miles to Junction City. If I'm going to play bloodhound, I'd better get started."

"A little man in a raincoat, a canvas hat, and carrying a Gladstone bag," Laurent murmured, repeating the description Trace had given in his story. "I don't envy you your task, Mr. Cooper, but let me know how you come out."

It must be true that nothing is really appreciated until it is lost; something had to account for the resentment Trace felt at Douglas Laurent's criticism of the ranch. But in that case, he reflected, he should be feeling awfully appreciative these days because losing things was fast becoming his only talent. And so now T. Cooper, the great loser, was setting out to find something—a man.

"I wonder where I would be if I were Steve Malone," he

48

mused, as Arthur headed the jeep back toward Mountain View.

Arthur grinned. "At a bar," he suggested.

"Now wait a minute, I said if I were Malone—" Trace paused and reflected a moment. "Say, you might have something there! I'll cover every bar in Junction City."

"In that case I'd better come along," Arthur sighed. "Somebody's got to cover you."

Arthur's concern was understandable, but Trace, oddly enough, didn't feel a bit thirsty. What he did feel was more like excitement. "Life gets dull without challenge," Laurent had said. "The mob says guilty, and so I must say innocent." But Trace knew it was more than that. He remembered Danny, the skinny legs in the tight levis, the close-cropped hair, the scared face. Danny Ross was all the people in the world who were strangers on earth, and for that reason he could be no stranger to Trace.

"I want to stop off and see the kid before we go on to Junction City," he said. "I want to let him know Laurent's in his corner."

But they were going to stop sooner than that. They were going to stop rather abruptly about ten miles beyond the ranch turnoff when a frantic, wild-eyed Virgil Keep suddenly appeared on the road ahead waving both arms like a windmill gone crazy.

"Where the hell have you been?" he yelled. "Why couldn't you be around when you're needed?"

The sheriff was alone; no Danny, no sedan. But he did have an ugly bruise on the side of his head.

"He tricked me!" Virgil roared. "He pulled the keys to stop the car and slugged me with my own gun. I knew that God-damned kid was a killer!"

Chapter Seven

All the little one-track trails led somewhere, but where they led was a mystery to Danny. Away—that's all he could think of now, just away. He was free. He had a steering wheel in his hands again and a powerful motor responding to the press of the accelerator. But he couldn't go back to the highway—not past that Mountain View crossing where a pair of armed deputies were watching for the return of the sheriff's sedan, and he certainly couldn't go back to Cooperton. He took the first trail cutting up from the south, praying that it wouldn't double back or run into the wall of a canyon. All directions had been lost on that twisting ride to the mine, but he knew that the mountains ran like twin walls, one to the east, one to the west, and the trick was to cut between them.

It was a desperate chance he'd taken, but desperate conditions breed desperate remedies. Virgil Keep had forgotten that. He knew Danny was afraid, just a scared, scrawny kid against a huge man with a gun riding on his hip; but the same fear that paralyzes can propel and so Danny was free.

But free for what? Gradually, as the minutes of freedom ticked off and the wretched road ground beneath the tires, reason returned. Freedom to run and hide, freedom to be hunted down like a dog, or to starve here on the desert. Danny began to remember things. He was broke. He didn't have the price of a sandwich, let alone that stake that was going to take him to faraway places. And now he was a fugitive, a name and a description that would soon be racing across the wires and airwaves to weave a tight net for a runaway in a stolen car. What did he have for a friend now? What did he have for an ally?

The answer lay on the seat beside him: the gun he'd ripped from the sheriff's holster when he grabbed for the keys. There was blood on the barrel from where it had ripped across a human skull, and the sight of it brought out the sweat beads on Danny's forehead. But he couldn't toss the dread object out the window as he wanted to. Now it was all he had.

Virgil was a miserable man when he rode back to Mountain View in a red jeep. It was tough enough to get that bash on the head, have the car stolen from under him, and lose a prisoner half his size without having to face a barrage of questions. The deputies knew better than to strain his temper; but Viola was a taxpayer with her tongue hung in the middle and loose at both ends, and Jim Rice's blue pickup was at the pumps getting gassed up. Jim wasn't exactly mute himself.

"Dammit, Virgil," he said, as soon as the story had been told, "that kid was locked up safe last night. Why did you let him out again?"

Virgil reddened. "We were looking for something," he said, "—for Charley Gaynor's wallet. The kid didn't have it on him, and Trace said—"

"Trace!"

Trace Cooper inspired various reactions from his neighbors. Some still respected him because he was a Cooper and they remembered his father or his grandfather; others despised him for identical reasons. Jim Rice wasn't one to be awed by a name.

"What the hell's Trace got to say about things?" he stormed. "Why don't he mind his own business?"

"Why don't you?" Trace parried.

"Do you think it's not my business when a killer's at large? I've got a family to think about, I've got a wife!"

That sympathetic murmur from Viola was too much for Trace. "Running away doesn't necessarily make the kid a killer," he said, "but I'm sure glad it makes you think of your wife, Jim. It's about time!"

The only thing that saved Trace from catching a faceful of knuckles was the size of Arthur standing at his shoulder— that and the way Virgil suddenly swung into action. Danny hadn't been free long—he couldn't have gotten far. The valley and the mountains were laced with little roads, some dead-end roads to ranches, some connecting with highways at distant points. The alarm had to be sent out and the search begun, and there was no place like Mountain View to begin.

"I need your truck, Jim," he said.

"Then you need me, too."

"Anyway you like it. Take one of the boys and start looking. Danny didn't come this way so he must have turned off somewhere between here and where he slugged me. That was about five miles back."

"I've got a car," Walter broke in. "It's not much but it runs."

"You're not going to leave me here alone!" Viola

51

screamed. "I don't want happening to me what happened to Francy Allen!"

"Francy!" Trace choked. "What's Danny Ross got to do with Francy?" But his question wasn't answered except for that knowing gleam in Viola's eyes. Virgil was too busy swinging into action. "One of the boys goes with Jim, one stays here in case the kid doubles back," he said. "As for me, I'm heading back to town to call the police at Junction City and Red Rock. . . . Ready, Trace?"

Virgil climbed back into the jeep again and Trace nodded. He felt sick inside at the thought of what was going out over that party line the instant Viola could get to the phone, and he felt even sicker at Jim Rice's parting words.

"Don't take it so hard, Trace," he taunted. "You'll find some other freak to add to your collection."

As Trace suspected, the news of Danny's escape reached Cooperton before them. A crowd was already gathering in front of the sheriff's office, but Virgil was all through offering explanations. "Drive around to the back door," he directed Arthur. "I haven't got time to make speeches." So Arthur swung the jeep around the corner and pulled into a little alleyway that led to the door of Ada's kitchen. Virgil issued no invitations, but Trace followed him inside.

At first the place seemed deserted, and then Ada came trotting in from the front of the building. Her face was flushed with excitement and her little eyes bright and anxious. "There's a lot of men waiting out front to see you," she panted. "And the phone keeps ringing—"

"That's fine!" Virgil snapped. "I'll probably have to chase every old hen in town off the line!" He started for the corridor to the office and then looked back to see Trace standing just inside the door. "Well, what do you want?" he demanded. "I don't need you any more."

"You don't need that crowd out front either," Trace said.

"What do you mean?"

"Sending Jim Rice out was all right, he has a deputy with him, but if you let that bunch form a vigilantes committee we may find Danny Ross at the end of a rope."

"Right now I don't care how we find him," Virgil said. "He took that chance when he broke loose. Remember, he's out there in the desert somewhere right now. He's desperate and he has my gun!"

"The poor boy," Ada murmured. "Where will he go?"

Even Virgil had no words for the disgust this comment brought to his eyes. "Talk to them," Trace urged. "Tell them to leave everything to the law. Tell them there's nothing in the crazy story Viola Wade's cooking up. That woman's just a natural troublemaker."

"It's her condition," Ada insisted. "She's going to have a baby—"

"What would you know about her condition?" Virgil cut in. "As for her crazy story, Trace, I guess you mean the way she keeps hollering about Francy's death. Well, for your information I can't tell them there's nothing in that. I don't know how Francy Allen died. . . . Do you?"

The stomp of Virgil's heavy footsteps could be heard all the way down the hall, and then the kitchen was as quiet as the end of time. Now Trace knew what he'd followed Virgil inside to find out. Somehow he'd known all the time.

"She died of sin," Ada murmured. "Everybody dies of sin."

. . . Everybody dies of sin. Trace carried the words with him all the way across town to a flat brick building with colored glass windows and a faded canopy running out to the street. You wouldn't think it to look at Cooperton now, but once it had been a thriving community, bigger than Red Rock to the north, grander than Junction City to the south. Then the thread of fortune slowly ran out. The mines, copper and lead and gold, closed down one by one, or settled down to a steady trickle of production; the railroads pulled up their tracks and retreated, and the transcontinental highways had no use for a has-been. But through it all, the first days, the boom days, and the latter days, Fisher's Mortuary stood like a red-brick monument to the fragility of man.

Two senior Fishers had already required the services of their own establishment. The current proprietor, representative of the third generation, was a small, graying man with yellowish skin and soft brown eyes. He greeted Trace as if he were a favored connoisseur entering an exclusive art gallery.

"She is beautiful, Mr. Cooper," he beamed. "I think you'll agree that I've followed your wishes completely."

Trace was a bit vague as to what was meant by these words. Yesterday was a soggy memory full of pain and regret, but the stale air of this drab waiting room brought back what he didn't want to remember. In this very spot he had stood ordering a funeral for Francy, pouring out more grief than any man would show without sufficient bourbon to dissolve his reticence; and then the door had opened behind him and Joyce had come in. She wasn't alone. Joyce was never alone if Lowell Glenn could reach her. The sight of them together was salt in an old wound.

"You can't come!" he shouted. "You're not invited to Francy's funeral!"

Sober, Trace would have caught the signal in Fisher's expressive eyes—but how could he know the old man was dead? All he knew, all he'd known for hours, was that Francy was gone where she couldn't be hurt any more. But now Joyce was staring at him with white horror in her face. Didn't she know? Hadn't she heard what was happening to Trace Cooper? The whole town knew he was nothing but a drunken bum; she had no right to look so stricken!

"Take a good look!" he said. "Be sure you know me the next time we meet!"

"Mr. Cooper," Fisher began, "you don't understand—"

"Of course I understand! Some women are good and some women are bad, that's all there is to understand. Do you know the difference, Fisher? The bad ones have a heart. The bad ones give what the good ones sell. . . ."

Trace didn't want to think about the rest. Like an automaton he followed Fisher through a draped doorway, not knowing or caring where they were going until it was too late. When they stopped, it was at the side of Francy's coffin.

"It's the best one I had, Mr. Cooper," the mortician explained. "And I sent down for that blue dress you mentioned. She looks real lifelike, doesn't she?"

The dead never looked lifelike to Trace . . . least of all Francy. She was too young to be lying there that way. She'd lived too little—or maybe too much in too little time. Just now Trace couldn't remember which year it was that

Francy had come to the ranch, but he'd been a youngster too tall for his trousers and she was a little tyke, newly orphaned, come to stay with her grandmother, the housekeeper. She was a gawky adolescent when he was at college, and belle of the high school when he went overseas. Whatever her age, she still looked as if she should be wearing ribbons in her yellow hair.

"I think I did a real nice job," Fisher commented. "The bruises hardly show."

Now Trace remembered what he'd come for: the bruises, the wound. "It was murder, wasn't it?" he asked.

Fisher looked frightened. "I couldn't say, Mr. Cooper. I just couldn't say."

"But suppose you could say? Nobody's going to quote you."

"Well, at first I thought it was an accident—one of those hit-and-run affairs, but after what happened to the doctor . . . I mean, there's a great similarity."

Trace knew exactly what he meant. Viola Wade wasn't the only imaginative person in the community; the conclusion she'd reached was probably becoming prevalent.

"What about the death certificate?" he asked. "Charley Gaynor must have signed one or you couldn't have taken Francy out of the hospital."

"That's filed in Red Rock . . . oh, I see what you mean. Charley was coroner for this area, wasn't he? He might have made a report. I guess Virgil will check on that. But you know, they're saying that boy might have been down here the night Francy was—well, whatever happened to her, and that he drove back toward Red Rock and wrecked his car to hide the bloodstains."

"Bloodstains?" Trace echoed. "What bloodstains . . . and what car?"

"His car—Danny Ross's. He told Virgil that he was driving a car that broke down yesterday morning so he shoved it over the grade and went on foot until Charley offered him a ride. That sounds fishy, doesn't it? They're saying he pushed it over and then came back this way as if he'd never been here before."

All the time he talked Fisher was fussing with Francy, straightening her dress, working at a blue smudge on the

fingers of her right hand. "Mean stuff to get off," he muttered, and Trace turned away. He didn't want to insult the
little man's artistry, but Francy didn't look lifelike at all. As
for the story he'd just heard, it was news to Trace—car and
all—but he had an old argument with whatever "they say."

"It might be a good idea to find that car before hanging
the kid twice," he muttered.

Outside, the sun was hanging up a record for the season,
and a bunch of noisy kids were playing baseball on a vacant
lot. Down the street a couple of high-school girls were gig-
gling their way to the drugstore for an afternoon Coke, and
everything was normal and alive.

Trace was shaking when he crawled up beside Arthur in
the jeep. He didn't want to go to Junction City. He wanted
to turn around and make a beeline for Murph's bar so he
could take up where he'd left off last night.

"Cut it out, Trace," Arthur said, switching on the ignition. "Stop blaming yourself for everything. You couldn't
help what happened to Francy."

Chapter Eight

After the first hour Danny began to let up on the accelerator. No one could drive that hard continually, not
even an expert hot rodder, and it wasn't easy to hold the
bouncing sedan on that washboard road. The first few
miles had been a series of twists and turns, but now the
narrow trail had straightened out to cut like an arrow across
the flat belly of the desert. The mountain walls still rose to
the east and the west, lower now or else farther away, but
nothing obstructed the view of that empty road before him.
Empty before and empty behind, with not a sign of pursuit.

At first it seemed good not to be followed. It was just that
kind of a road, and he was being lucky for a change; but
then Danny began to worry. What if he had hit the sheriff
too hard? What if he wasn't being followed simply because
no one had yet found the body? Such a thought was

enough to bring that speedometer down another twenty points and put a chill on the air in that steaming sedan. Then Danny remembered the radio and turned a switch on the dashboard. He didn't have long to wait.

". . . is believed to be heading south toward the border," the announcer was saying, "probably on the Junction City road." A dip in the road faded out the voice momentarily, but Danny knew who the announcer was talking about. "We repeat, this man is armed," the voice resumed. "He has escaped custody of the sheriff at Cooperton and is fleeing in the sheriff's car, license number—"

Danny automatically resumed speed. The more that voice talked, the faster he drove. Now it was the description, the very picture of Danny Ross in his faded levis and leather jacket called out as if he were being set up for auction. Sold to the highest bidder, only don't get too close because this kid's a killer—this kid has a gun. They were going to give Danny ideas if they kept broadcasting that stuff. He shut off the radio. It was hard enough to think without that noise.

". . . believed to be heading south." Those were the words that stuck in his mind. He was heading south all right, due south, and now this empty road had suddenly become a trap. No wonder he wasn't being followed! This road had only two ends—he couldn't get away! As sure as sin there was a road block ahead; as sure as fate there was another behind him, and it seemed a little silly to be hurrying so fast into the arms of the law.

Danny slammed on the brakes and came to a screeching stop. He was afraid to go on. Any moment now that shimmering screen of heat on the road before him might turn into a dust cloud full of police cars. They would move in to take him in daylight most likely, and there was plenty of it left. They would close in from both ends without a chance of missing since the road had no turnoffs and no hiding places. Danny squinted at the sun-baked terrain all about him: flat, treeless, with no growth at all except the sparse desert brush. No hiding place for a man, let alone a stolen car. But sometime back he'd caught a glimpse of what appeared to be a dry river off to the east. A river meant a riverbank, and that meant something to use for shelter if it could be reached. It was worth a try anyway, so he shifted into low and twisted the steering wheel.

That washboard road he'd been fretting about was velvet compared to no road at all. The wheels spun in the deep dust, the little sedan groaned, shuddered, and then took off across the desert like a skittish mare breaking tether. A plume of dust rose up behind the car, a directing finger for any curious eye, but Danny was still as alone as if creation had just begun.

The river was a lot closer than he had expected—he had to slam the brakes on quick to keep from racing right over the edge of its ragged ravine. With the brake set, he crawled out cautiously to look about for some more shallow approach. There was no vegetation and no possible way of hiding the sedan except on the river bed, and the road was still in sight if he squinted against the sun. The empty road. The silent road. Danny cocked his head and listened. Silent? That wasn't the desert drone he heard in the distance, rising, throbbing, coming nearer. For a moment he feared it was a plane and there was no hiding place at all from a plane, but the sky was innocent of this violation. Now there was no time to worry about the fate of the sedan. Danny reached in and grabbed the gun from the seat and then released the hand brake and let gravity take care of the rest.

The dust had completely settled by the time the car on the road came into view. Flattened against the wall of the riverbank, Danny peeked over the edge and watched it pass. It was too far away to be sure, but from the length of aerial the sunlight played upon it sure looked like a police car. He didn't really breathe until it was out of sight and the last echo of the motor had faded away in the south. For once Lady Luck had been on his shoulder; if only she'd decide to hang around!

As Danny suspected, the road he had taken was blockaded, but so were all the other roads in the area. The state police, local peace officers, ranchers, and townspeople all joined in the search for old Charley Gaynor's killer, because now there was no doubt of it. An innocent man didn't cut and run no matter what darned fools like Trace Cooper said, and a good man hunt beat riding fence or swapping gossip at the barbershop any day.

By midafternoon, at about the same time Danny was sliding down that ravine and fixing to follow the river south, Jim Rice stomped into Virgil Keep's office, hot, tired, and profane. "Goddamit, Virgil, I blew a tire," he stormed. "Blew a practically new six-ply on a damn chuckhole. I ain't going to pay for it. I'm putting in a bill and the county can pay for it!"

"Keep your shirt on," Virgil said. "What about Danny Ross? See anything of him?"

"How could I? All I saw was a lot of ruts and dust. Don't they ever grade roads around here? It's a wonder I didn't snap an axle."

"Roads aren't in my department," Virgil muttered.

"Well, I guess that's one thing to be grateful for!"

If looks could kill Jim Rice's wife would have been a widow right then. Virgil leaped up from the desk he'd been jockeying all afternoon and swung Jim around to face the large map of the county hanging on the wall. "Look," he bellowed, thumping the map with a thick forefinger, "look for yourself and see how much chance that kid has of getting away. I've got the Junction City police blocking the main road to the south, the Red Rock police to the north and every available state police car covering every road in between. In addition, every deputy on my force is out searching and so is half of Cooperton. Ross can either keep going until he runs into a road block or stay out there until he starves; but he sure as hell can't get away!"

"Unless he has help," Rice murmured.

Virgil stopped tapping the map long enough to pick up that very special connotation. "Who's going to help him?" he demanded.

"Who helped him this morning?"

"You think Trace—?"

"Where is he?" Rice asked. "I stopped by his place on my way in, thinking I'd use his phone to call home. He ain't there. That big nigger ain't there. Not a living thing on Trace's place but that pack of mongrel dogs he keeps."

"He's probably out looking for Danny."

"That's what I figured," Jim grinned. "Only maybe Trace knows where to look."

It didn't take an old lady with an ouija board to see that Jim Rice wasn't very fond of Trace, and Virgil knew why. Jim and Trace had been kids together, one a rich man's son and the other as poor as patches, and Jim would be less than human not to enjoy seeing that spoiled brat brought to heel. But maybe there was more to it than that. "Wait a minute," Virgil called as Jim eased off toward the door. "There's something I've been wanting to ask you."

Jim frowned. "Well?"

"I hear you had dinner at the Pioneer Hotel night before last."

"That's right. Me and a cattle buyer from Red Rock."

"Francy Allen wait on your table by any chance?"

"Francy?" The red began to creep up around Jim's ears. "Francy quit working at the Pioneer long ago. You know that. Hell, it was your idea!"

"It wasn't my idea," Virgil corrected. "It's just my job to enforce the law. Francy was seen at your table the other night just the same. Maybe she was just helping you entertain that cattle buyer."

"She was tight. Can I help it if a woman drinks too much and hangs around my table?"

Jim Rice's voice had a way of getting higher and higher the more excited he became. "Then you didn't see her later?" Virgil asked, and in a near soprano Jim squeaked, "See her later? Virgil, I'm a married man!"

"That's not what I asked you. Did you see Francy Allen after you left the hotel, yes or no?"

"Of course not!"

There was about thirty seconds of silence after Jim's denial and then a crash. A crash and a splintering of glass that whirled both men about to face the hall door. There they found Ada, her bright, brown eyes fixed on Jim's face and a little empty space between her hands where the canning jar had been. "Oh," she murmured. "I dropped it!"

"What the hell are you doing in here?" Virgil stormed. "Can't you make a big enough mess in the kitchen without wrecking my office too?"

"It's watermelon preserve," Ada said. "I heard Jim's voice and remembered how much Ethel liked my watermelon preserve—"

"Well, don't just stand there, clean it up!"

Virgil turned around to continue his interrogation, but by this time Jim's back was disappearing through the doorway to the street. It was probably just as well. One problem at a time, Virgil figured, and right now the problem was Danny Ross. He studied the map again and tried to reassure himself. No, it couldn't be; no one could escape a net that tight. The mountains were full of trails and ranch roads, but the only two routes open to the south were bottled up tight. And the kid was heading south. Why else had he carried a Spanish dictionary?

But Jim Rice's accusation stuck in Virgil's mind. It wasn't like Trace to meddle the way he'd been doing all day unless he had a good reason for thinking Danny innocent. A real good reason . . .

When it began to turn dusk, Danny crawled up out of the river bed and tried to get his bearings. The sunset had left a dull red glow behind the ragged shadow of the western range, and a come-early moon in the east was getting a jump on the darkness. Moonlight was something Danny could appreciate under certain circumstances and with suitable company, but tonight he wanted darkness, black darkness with nothing but the stars to guide him. Stumbling along in that dusty river bottom all afternoon had given him time to make plans. He'd made quite a study of that road map that had gone over the side with the jalopy and remembered every town all the way down to the border. Junction City was about a hundred miles, maybe more, maybe less, below Cooperton, and he must have driven almost that far before dumping the sheriff's sedan. How far he had walked was something else again. Three or four miles at most with time out for an occasional cigarette from that dwindling pack Trace Cooper had tossed him in the cell. A few wilted cigarettes, part of a pack of matches, and a loaded gun—that was the extent of Danny's possessions. That and his plan.

There was a reason for calling it Junction City: the

east-west highway crossed the road from Cooperton there, and that meant, if he walked far enough, Danny was sure to hit the highway sooner or later and hit it in open country where no cops would be waiting. From a safe distance he could follow the lights of the traffic, or maybe even steal a ride on a truck at some roadside stop. As he walked, it grew darker until the moon, a little flat on one side, went to work. The wind came up too, and after a while the leather jacket he'd sweltered in all day began to feel good again. Then he saw it: the first beam of light racing across the dark horizon. The highway at last!

. . . Danny rode into Junction City on a trailer of shiny new automobiles bound for Los Angeles. It was the easiest hitch he'd ever made—the only tough part being crouching there in the darkness waiting for the driver and smelling the steaks sizzling in that roadside café he'd stopped to pa- tronize. On the way to town Danny figured an answer to that problem too. Anything was possible as long as he had that gun in his jacket, and there was nothing like necessity to supply a lack of nerve.

The crossing of the highways at Junction City was swarming with cops, but they were watching for a desper- ate kid in a stolen police car; they weren't interested in a load of new automobiles. The truck stopped for the signal, waited, and then crawled forward, but now it was about a hundred and forty pounds lighter, and Danny was halfway down the block. From here on he was traveling in style, chauffeur driven no less, but first he had to find the chauf- feur and a suitable limousine.

Junction City wasn't much of a town—two or three thou- sand population, Danny judged, and most of that went to bed with the chickens. But not all of it, not quite all. A few neons were keeping the street lights company: a couple of cafés, a few bars, a hole-in-the-wall movie house featuring a B-grade western. Danny wandered around town a while making his selection, and then he spotted something that was like a special delivery from Lady Luck. That bright spot just ahead was a drive-in restaurant. He crept closer. A drive-in with exactly one car pulled up for service, and that one a nice four-door sedan with only the driver inside. . . . Danny waited until the pretty car hop took the man's order, and then helped himself to the back seat.

"This is a gun in the back of your neck, mister," he said. "It goes off if you yell."

The light from the drive-in spilled over the man's face, and Danny watched it in the rear-view mirror: round, flabby, and stark white. It was good to see somebody else scared for a change.

"Wha—what do you want?" the man gasped.

"I'm not particular," Danny said. "I'll just take whatever you're having. You need to go on a diet anyway."

But now fat face was remembering and remembering fast. "Wait a minute," he said. "I know who you are. I heard about you on the radio. You're the one they're looking for!"

"I'm the one," Danny admitted, "so I don't have much to lose, do I? On the other hand, maybe you do. It all depends on what you say to that car hop when she comes back."

"I won't say a word!"

"Oh, yes, you will. You'll be just as friendly as you were being when I first spotted you, and I'll be down on the floor with this gun trained on the back of your head just in case you forget."

If he kept on talking that way Danny was going to feel as brave as he sounded. And everything worked out just as he said it would, even to the conversation.

"Ham on white, apple pie a la mode, and black coffee," the girl announced, fastening the tray on the window ledge. "I'm sorry but we're all out of chocolate."

"Vanilla is fine," the fat man answered. "Vanilla is just dandy!"

"Was there anything else?"

Danny waited, his finger on the trigger. The trouble with being on the floor was that he couldn't see much—just the back of the fat man's neck. He couldn't see any facial expressions or hand signals, and he didn't like that long silence following the car hop's question. He started to raise his head and just at that instant the loud-speaker from the drive-in cut loose with a brassy beat from the juke box inside. Brassy and loud and full of jump.

"Oh, God," moaned the car hop, "there he goes again— that same piece over and over!"

"Something wrong?" the fat man asked weakly.

"Just some customer we've had hanging around for the last couple nights. Some bum all liquored up and crazy about that one record. I simply can't stand it again! I'm going to shut off the loud-speaker. . . ."

The girl's voice died away, but the music went right on going to town. Now Danny knew what it was, low down and wide open and a long way from Basin Street. Some customer, she'd said! Some customer who didn't like western music? Some customer in a canvas hat and a wrinkled raincoat? Danny was up from the floor in an instant, his anxious eyes staring holes through that windshield. Three or four patrons were scattered about the circular counter clearly visible through the wide plate-glass windows, and one of them had to be Steve Malone!

When Malone finally left the drive-in, probably by request, the fat man's sedan was backed away in the shadows (the tray long since emptied and collected) anxiously awaiting further instructions. Danny didn't mind the wait because it gave him time to figure things out. If he kept going, he might make it to the border and he might not, but one way or the other he'd still be a murderer as long as he lived. But inside that building was a man who had the right answers. Of course he wouldn't talk voluntarily, but if a gun could make a dummy out of this boy in the front seat, why couldn't the same gun make Malone conversational? Aside from clearing his own name, Danny had a little matter of a personal score to settle. It wasn't nice to kill an old man, swipe his wallet, and then leave the next poor sucker who came along to take the rap!

By the time the glass doors swung open Danny's mind was made up. The man in the raincoat was the same one he'd seen at Mountain View, no doubt about it, and wherever he was going Danny was going too. The gun in his hand swung up and came down hard on the fat man's head. For this trip he didn't need a chauffeur.

Chapter Nine

Danny wasn't the only outsider visiting Junction City that night. Had he walked a few blocks below the drive-in, down where the store fronts weren't so modern and the street lamps were few and far between, he might have recognized the red jeep parked at the curbing and the big Negro in a white suit who was slumped over the steering wheel. Arthur was waiting for Trace, and Trace was out following a will-o'-the-wisp that eluded him from bar to bar. His question was always the same, and so was the answer.

"A little guy in a raincoat? A stranger? Does he hate western music, mister?"

Not knowing anything about Malone's musical tastes, Trace couldn't say. But he did keep following that lead, and it got hotter all the time.

"A little guy in a raincoat? Say, I had to throw out a fella like that last night. He got liquored up and tried to wreck my music box."

"How was he fixed for money?" Trace wanted to know.

"Oh, he had money, plenty of money. But I couldn't have him throwing bottles at the record machine!"

From bar to bar the lead grew hotter. It had to be Malone, Trace was certain of that, and then he got another idea. A drunk out on the town and loaded with cash would get around to women sooner or later, if they didn't get to him first, and it wasn't too difficult to follow that trail. It lead to a cheap hotel, an ancient frame structure in a run-down section of town, where he found a red-eyed night clerk dozing behind the desk and an old-fashioned register open on the counter. Half a dozen words with the night clerk and Trace returned to Arthur in the jeep.

"Well, I've found him," he announced. "At least I've found where he's staying; he's out right now."

Arthur turned up the collar of his jacket and hunched down deeper behind the wheel. "I suppose that means we just sit here and wait."

"I suppose it does."

"Look here, Trace, why don't you just telephone Laurent and tell him you've located his man? Maybe he has time for this stuff, but we have a place to look after."

Arthur knew it was a waste of lung power. Something had gotten into Trace ever since his first talk with Laurent, something good or something bad, Arthur was no judge, but whatever it was had kept him sober for twenty-four hours. Considering the number of bars he'd visited in the last three or four of them, that was quite remarkable.

"I can't do that," Trace explained. "In the first place, putting a call through the Cooperton office would be the same as hiring a sound truck and parading up and down Main Street. We want to keep Malone to ourselves. Besides, Laurent wouldn't come down here. He hasn't left the ranch half a dozen times in the past five years!"

"Smart man," Arthur muttered.

"You bet he's a smart man, and he didn't get that way running a tractor!"

Trace began to shuffle his feet on the sidewalk; he was restless, maybe from the smell of all those bars. But Arthur knew better than to say anything. He'd been tagging along after this boy too long not to have learned when to keep his mouth shut.

"I think I'll have another look around," Trace said. "I may run into him."

"You may miss him."

"Maybe, but you won't. You can see the hotel from here. Just keep your eye peeled for a little guy in a raincoat and a canvas hat."

Trace drifted off and was soon lost beyond the dull glow of the corner street lamp. None of Junction City's streets had much in the way of illumination, but this one looked as if somebody had instituted a budget drive on the light bill. The only bright spot was the neon over a bowling alley a couple of doors down, that and the yellow mouth of the hotel doorway. Arthur swung about sideways and planted his feet on the seat. That way he could watch the hotel and get a little rest. It had been a long, futile day, and his lids were getting awfully heavy. . . .

He awakened with a start. There were footsteps coming

out of the darkness, unsteady, stumbling footsteps coming up the wavy sidewalk. Arthur sat up and blinked his eyes. A man came into view, a little man in a wrinkled raincoat that was unbuttoned and flapping crazily in the night wind. He was taking about two steps crosswise for every one step ahead, but even at that erratic pace he made it to the hotel. Arthur began to look about for some sign of Trace, and that's when he caught sight of the shadow trailing Malone: a furtive shadow, long and skinny and hugging the buildings as if fearful of being seen. But the light from the hotel window caught him in bold relief—a kid in jeans and a leather jacket!

One look and Arthur forgot all about Malone. "Hey," he yelled, vaulting out of the jeep, "hey, you! Wait a minute!"

The shadow responded by taking off like a scared rabbit.

Danny had followed Malone all the way from the drive-in, a crazy, zigzag route that wasn't easy on the nerves. Maybe Malone had all the time in the world to get where he was going, but Danny didn't. Sooner or later that tap he'd given the fat man was going to wear off, and when that happened the alarm would be out all over town. Before that happened he wanted a chance to pin this boy down somewhere and have a little chat over a gun barrel; but first they had to stop at a liquor store for a bottle this drunk certainly didn't need, and then go on to this dark, empty street. . . . But suddenly it wasn't empty any more.

At the sound of the voice Danny flattened against the side of the building and momentarily froze in his tracks. He couldn't see who it was calling him—the street light between them got in his eyes—but a voice that big must belong to a cop. He spun about and started running, and the man behind him started running too.

A head start and the incentive of fear gave Danny an edge in the race, and the unpaved alleyway that loomed up in the darkness didn't hurt a bit. He cut the corner sharply, doubled back at the first crossing, and scrambled over the top of the highest fence he came to. A fence like that was sure to discourage pursuit from anyone less agile. Crouched in the shadows between a couple of trash cans he miraculously avoided, he waited for the footsteps. They didn't come. He'd lost the pursuer, whoever he was, but he didn't dare come out of hiding too soon. It could be a trap, or the man might have gone for re-enforcements.

After a few minutes, when the thumping of his heart had slowed down a bit, Danny began looking about him. It was a noisy place he'd come to: the back yard of a bowling alley where from the sound of things they must have been holding a tournament. He could hear each ball as it sped down the alley, hear the pins drop, and almost tally the score. They must have bowled several frames while he crouched there waiting for footsteps and trying to get his bearings.

It wasn't much of a neighborhood. Next door to the bowling alley he could make out the square hulk of a two-story building with an iron fire escape threading down its back wall and a lot of windows, some dark, some light. One of the dark ones turned light as Danny watched, and a man came over and raised the sash. He was still wearing his raincoat and canvas hat.

So Danny had doubled back to the hotel again! That was a real break, and right about now he could use a few. With the cover of crashing pins behind him he didn't have to worry too much about making noise while looking about for some access to the next yard. There must be a service entrance to the hotel and that meant a way to get up to Malone without risking the street again. He took another look at that bright window, fixing its location in his mind: second floor rear, third window from the end.

When Danny shinnied up that fence and back into the alley, the only sign of life was an amber-eyed tomcat sampling the fare of the garbage cans. He didn't bother the cat, and the cat didn't bother him—but something else did. A shadow where no shadow had been before, a gleam of reflected light where no light had shown. Danny edged forward and banged his knees against a low bumper, and then a gate creaked somewhere in the darkness, sending him back behind the tomcat's garbage can. Much as he wanted to peek out, he dared not. That car parked behind the hotel probably carried a couple of cops that were a lot more anxious to see Danny Ross than he was to see them. He waited until there was a low purring sound that didn't belong to anything feline, and then stepped out to find the shadow gone.

At least now he knew where to find the gate. The rest was easy. The gate stood open, and whoever had used that rear door to the hotel had been thoughtful enough to leave it unlocked. The narrow hall inside was conveniently dark and empty, and from the lighted lobby just ahead came the sound of heavy snoring. The front way was probably safe enough, but Danny didn't need a room number now. He found the service stairs and went up quietly.

. . . Second floor rear, third window from the end. Third window must mean third door as well, because this was no luxury spot with cross ventilation and a view of the mountains. It was dark and dismal, the kind of place where another bum groping down the hall would never be noticed even if he did have a lump in his throat and a gun in his hand. What Danny expected from Malone was nothing but trouble—no man puts his head in a noose willingly—but with all that liquor in him he might talk without knowing what he was doing. The whisky smell was overpowering even from the hall, and he really didn't expect an answer to that stealthy knock. The door was unlocked, and Danny wasn't bashful now.

The light was still burning in that shabby room, a naked bulb that dangled from the ceiling like one bright eye fixed and staring at a man flat on his back on the bed. He was still wearing the raincoat, its tails spread out like a fan, and the canvas hat was crumpled over his face. Beside him was an old-fashioned pocketbook turned inside out so its contents spilled over the mattress: a few coins, a couple of dirty cards, and a whole fistful of crumpled twenty-dollar bills. The bills were all Danny could see.

"Malone," he choked, "get up. Goddamit, get up!"

But when he snatched the hat away, Malone just stared at the ceiling with empty eyes, and a little stream of blood trickled out of the hole in his forehead.

Chapter Ten

How long Danny stood there pointing that gun at a dead man was something he would never know—long enough for all his hopes to perish, long enough to lose all sense of reality. Malone was dead, and that didn't figure. All this time he'd thought of the little man in the raincoat as the old doctor's murderer, but as a murderer this body on the bed made no sense unless it was a case of remorse and suicide. Remorse was hardly the word for the happy drunk he'd followed to this hotel, and suicide by means of a bullet in the head was a bit difficult for a man without a weapon. . . . Malone had no gun. He had an unopened fifth still clutched in one hand; he had the old Gladstone bag, opened and in a state of wild disarray on the floor; and he had the clutter from that emptied pocketbook on the mattress. Anything else he possessed was in the nature of knowledge, and a dead man has no memory.

The maple pins spilling over in the bowling alley again brought Danny to his senses. They made a perfect cover for the sound of a shot, and the shot that silenced Malone hadn't been fired so long ago. He tried to put into minutes the time that had passed since he crouched in the yard next door and watched a man in a raincoat raise the window. It didn't matter. It never mattered how close a miss was, it was a miss just the same; but what did matter was the memory of that creaking gate and the car that was and then suddenly wasn't in the alley. The police? That's what Danny had taken for granted at the time, but would a cop sneak in and out the back way when all he had to do was march up to the desk and flash a badge?

Danny suddenly felt terribly conspicuous. He was standing in the middle of a brightly lighted room, a gun in his hand, and a brand-new corpse on the bed. The full significance of Malone's sudden departure from the earth might take time to understand, but this was no place for meditation. Soon the police would come, very soon because now

Danny remembered a terrible thing. The fat man at the drive-in had seen Malone too, and by this time he must have given a vivid description to be relayed to every cop in town. It didn't take second sight to predict what they would make of this body on the bed.

Even as the thought hit him he picked up the sound of footsteps in the hall. So soon? Was he to have no chance at all? The window was no good—it was nowhere near the fire escape—and the closet was the first place anyone would look. But now there was a knocking nobody would answer, and then the turning of the doorknob. His only chance was to stand behind the door when it opened and pray for a break. . . .

But it wasn't the law that walked into Malone's room. It was a redheaded man in a wrinkled suit.

Trace Cooper was the last person Danny expected to see—in this room or anywhere else. He'd figured Trace to be just a guy who'd gone along for the ride until it got boring, and then took off down a mountain trail without so much as a "go to hell" to the kid he was leaving alone with a sadistic sheriff. Cooper belonged over a hundred miles away, bending an elbow probably, but here he was walking into Malone's room as casually as if he'd made an appointment.

He walked as far as the bed and froze in his tracks. Danny had let the crumpled hat fall to the floor after uncovering Malone's face, and nothing hid the story now. Trace took it all in: the little man in the raincoat with the ventilated head, the empty pocketbook, the wad of currency on the bed. He even moved closer and straightened out each wrinkled bill—Danny counted seven of them—and then felt for some sign of pulse. That was silly; anybody could see Malone was beyond telling tales.

Suddenly Danny saw the light—tales, that was it! Malone had been around to the men's room at Mountain View just about the time the old doctor must have been killed. He might have witnessed the murder and cut and run to save his own skin, or he might have seen someone leaving in enough of a hurry to make his knowledge dangerous. He had money, sure, but without serial numbers a twenty-dollar bill was just a twenty-dollar bill. It was all Danny could do to keep from blurting out his new-found wisdom; but now Trace was moving about, poking at that untidy suitcase on the floor, opening and closing the empty dresser drawers, and displaying the attitude of a man not so much taken by surprise as annoyed by some small thing he couldn't put his finger on. But the dresser had a mirror, and the mirror had a reflection.

Trace's back stiffened. "You crazy fool!" he said. "Put that damned gun away before somebody gets hurt!"

Danny had forgotten the thing in his hand. It did look conspicuous in view of that body on the bed.

"I didn't shoot him!" he sputtered. "He was like that when I got here!"

"And when was that?"

"Just before you came in. Just a couple of minutes ago."

Trace turned about slowly, and the question in his eyes didn't make his meeting any cozier. "And how did you get here?" he asked. "How did you know where to find Malone?"

It was a loaded question, and Danny's denial was quick. "I didn't know. I saw him on the street and followed him."

"Just now?"

"A little while ago. But when I started to turn into the hotel somebody hollered at me. I thought it was a cop and started running. I just now got back."

Trace was listening. Whether or not he was buying this story was another question, but he was listening. "If you're not going to shoot me, would you mind pointing that gun some other way?" he said. "It makes me nervous."

"It makes me nervous too," Danny retorted.

"What does that mean?"

"It means you're not going to turn me in. I've got troubles enough with one murder I didn't do; I'm not going to be stuck with this one!"

"With this?" A crooked grin played about Trace's mouth. He stepped over to the bed again and scrutinized the hole in Malone's head. It was a small hole, neat and round and colored with blood and powder burns. "With that blunderbuss of Virgil's you'd have blown his head off at such short range," he said. "Now suppose we stop trying to scare each other and find out what happened here. This man hasn't been dead long."

Maybe it was just a line to put Danny off guard, or maybe he really didn't suspect the obvious. Danny had a few questions of his own he wanted to ask—what Trace was doing here, for instance, and how he'd known where to find Steve Malone—but he wouldn't ask them. Instead he'd go into that story about seeing Malone from the yard next door, and tell about the car in the alley and the creaking gate. He would have rehearsed his whole day if there'd been time, because that's how it was with Trace Cooper. He gave you a grin and a couple of encouraging words, and you poured your heart out.

"How long ago was all this?" Trace wanted to know, and Danny was trying to figure that, too, when a siren wailed out of the distance and he started like a scared colt. Even Trace couldn't blot out the facts of death.

"Expecting somebody?" Trace asked. A body on the bed didn't seem to mean a thing.

"I've got to get out of here!" Danny said. "I almost forgot—I slugged a guy down at a drive-in."

"You what?"

"I slugged him. I had this gun on him and was going to make him drive me over the border. Then I spotted Malone and decided to follow him instead."

At least Trace didn't need a diagram to get the idea. "Bright boy!" he cried, heading toward the door. "Keeping you from hanging yourself is going to be the toughest case Laurent ever took on."

That was the first Danny heard of Alexander Laurent, and although the name added to his collection of questions in need of an answer, there was no time for conversation now. They were back in that dark hall with the door closed on Malone's last drunk when the siren and the police car behind it made a simultaneous halt in front of the hotel. Trace peeked over the front stair railing and drew back quickly. "Where's that back stair?" he whispered, but Danny was already leading the way. They could hear loud voices waking up the bewildered night clerk as they slipped out the back way, and there was no time for anything but breathing until they reached the black alley behind the hotel.

73

But the alley was a long way from a point of safety. "Maybe I can slip around and catch Arthur's attention," Trace suggested, but the gun Danny was still using for courage got in his way. When the chips were down, Danny trusted nobody, even if it meant hiding in alleys all night. Where Trace went he was going, sensible or not. It was an impasse, and they were stuck with it until a flat-nosed vehicle slid into view at the end of the alley.

"Arthur!" Trace yelled, and took off at a sprint with Danny on his heels. It was the first time either of them had seen a delivering angel in a jeep, but on a night such as this anything was possible.

It was almost twelve hours to the minute from the time Danny had parted company with Virgil Keep that he was back on the road to Cooperton—and under protest since his own wish was to head for the border. "Haven't you pulled enough boners for one day?" Trace objected. "Don't you know that's exactly where you're expected?" Partly because of this logic, and mostly because Arthur seemed no more impressed by the gun than his companion, Danny acquiesced. Arthur wasn't favorably impressed by any part of this operation, and that was natural enough. Whisking a fugitive away from the outstretched arms of the law was a dangerous pastime, and Arthur's ancestors weren't distinguished pioneers of anything but a marked lack of privilege. It was he who insisted on the bottom of the back seat for Danny, and on the heavy tarpaulin that transformed him into a shapeless lump on the floor boards.

That was how they left Junction City, with the sirens screaming up in the darkness behind them, and the network of police cars getting the radioed message that Danny Ross had struck again. And so the way was cleared for them, and the road back to Cooperton left as empty and open as Trace had expected.

Once they were rid of the city Danny crawled out of the tarpaulin and looked around. The moon was still up, and the sky had an epidemic of stars. The whole earth seemed as peaceful and quiet as if the troublesome part of creation had never been made, and strange unnatural acts like murder couldn't happen. But murder had happened—twice in two days—and nobody concerned with this affair could fail to see a certain significance in Steve Malone's death. But to Danny that significance was one thing; to another man, Arthur Jackson, for instance, it could be something quite different.

"You're playing with dynamite," Danny heard him tell Trace. "Why do you suppose Malone was killed?"

"An interesting question," Trace murmured. "Maybe he saw something back at Mountain View."

"That's what I was thinking, and maybe what he saw was Danny Ross. Have you thought of that?"

Danny hadn't thought of it, but the moment Arthur spoke the words he knew it was going to be a popular idea. "It's a possibility," Trace conceded. ". . . Oh, hello. Are you back with that thing again?" He'd turned halfway around and was looking at Danny, sitting on the edge of the back seat now with that gun pointed straight ahead. "If we hit a bump, and I promise you we will, that gadget's liable to go off and then who'll get you out of this mess?"

"Is that what you're supposed to be doing," Danny asked.

"That's what I am doing. Did you ever hear of a man named Alexander Laurent? No, of course you didn't. Laurent hasn't practiced for five years, and five years ago you probably weren't reading newspapers except to follow the Tigers."

"The Cubs," Danny corrected, and Trace cocked a shaggy red eyebrow at him. It wasn't a very smart remark from a kid who claimed to be from Detroit.

"Alexander Laurent," Trace continued, "is one of the greatest criminal lawyers of all time. He never lost a capital case in over a hundred trials, and he could name his own fee anywhere in the country. But then five years ago Laurent retired and bought a ranch about ten miles from Mountain View."

Trace fell silent for a moment. "What does that make me?" Danny demanded.

"About the luckiest guy in the world. You see, Danny, Alexander Laurent knows all about you, and he doesn't think you killed Charley Gaynor. He's on your side, with me working as middle man—that's why you're with us right now instead of in the Junction City jail."

Now Danny recalled that crack of Trace's when they made the quick exit from Malone's hotel. Other things added up too: the way this jeep had followed him around all morning, and the way it disappeared about ten miles from Mountain View.

"Is that where you went this morning?" he asked, and Trace nodded.

"He's a smart man, Danny," he said. "He put me on to looking for Malone in Junction City. I just followed a trail of bars until I came to that hotel; but I sure didn't expect to find you there."

"Or Malone dead," Arthur muttered. "But maybe Alexander the Great can dope that out over an iced mint julep."

"Wait a minute," Danny broke in, "what's this all about anyway? I haven't any money for a lawyer. I haven't anything but that two hundred the sheriff took off me yesterday."

"Laurent doesn't want your money," Trace said.

"Then what does he want?"

"The truth. The answer to who did kill Dr. Gaynor."

That lopsided moon sliding over toward one black wall of mountains brought Trace's troubled frown out of the darkness. It was the same expression Danny had seen back in Malone's room when he was adding up all those zeros. "I wonder what Raney pays a common laborer for two weeks' work," he murmured, and there wasn't going to be any answer because Trace was talking to himself. But he wasn't talking to himself when he asked, "Think back, Danny, did you see Malone talking to anybody back at Mountain View? Did he talk to the doctor, for instance?"

"How should I know," Danny answered. "They both went out before I did."

"And so did Jim Rice?"

"Sure, that's what I told the sheriff. What are you driving at?"

"I haven't any idea," Trace confessed. "All I know is that Steve Malone had a hundred and forty dollars in twenty-dollar bills, and from the looks of things he must have spent plenty before we got there. But he didn't have old Charley's wallet. I've seen that wallet."

"He probably chucked it," Arthur suggested. "What's the difference anyway?"

"A little matter of evidence, for one thing. If we could find that wallet someplace where Danny has never been—"

"It's a big country," Arthur said.

It was a big country all right. Big and wide and lonely—and frightening, like those scenes painted on the walls of the dinosaur room in the Field Museum. Danny crawled back in the tarpaulin again, as if the night was really as icy as it seemed at the moment. Nobody had to paint pictures for Danny Ross. He knew the hole he was in was a lot deeper now than it had been a dozen hours ago. If only Trace had told him about Laurent sooner! If only he'd known it was more than just himself against the world! But was it really? He balanced the gun in his right hand, and the weight of it still made him feel better than anything Trace had said. He'd keep it handy anyway just in case they tried any funny business at Cooperton. . . .

It was long after midnight when the signboard with the population figures showed up on the shoulder. The only lights showing were a few widely spaced naked bulbs hung overhead across the highway, because at this hour Cooperton was as dead as a churchyard—and it had one of those too.

"Remember, you two," Danny called up to the front seat, "you're not turning me over to that sheriff!"

Trace yawned. He'd slept most of the way in, and came out of his slumber with much stretching of arms. "Relax," he murmured. "I've got just the hiding place for you."

"Not the farm!" Arthur insisted. "If Virgil finds out you were in Junction City tonight, that's the first place he'll look."

"You give Virgil entirely too much credit—"

Trace got no farther. It was exactly then that Arthur slammed on the brakes and Danny fell on his face to the floor boards. "Keep your head down!" Trace muttered as he started to rise, and a heavy hand on the top of his head added persuasion to the directive. But not before Danny caught a glimpse of what had caused the sudden stop. They were just even with the cemetery, but that wasn't a stone figure pinned in the beam of the headlights; it was a woman.

"Oh, Mr. Cooper! You gave me such a start!"

The Cooper came out Cupper, but Danny would have recognized Ada's voice anyway. Everything she said sounded like an apology.

"You gave us a fright too," Trace said. "We weren't expecting pedestrians at this hour. What are you up to anyway?"

"I couldn't sleep," Ada answered. "Lately I don't sleep well at all, and it seems such a waste of time just to go on tossing and turning when it's so nice outside. Have you noticed how lovely the mockingbirds sing these nights, Mr. Cooper?"

"I can't say that I have."

"You should. We miss so much out of life by just not noticing things."

There were a few things Danny would just as soon Ada didn't notice right now; a few lumps under the canvas in the back seat. He was hoping Arthur would get the jeep rolling again, but Trace had to go right on making conversation. "Does Virgil know you're out?" he asked.

"Heavens, no! He's away looking for that poor boy. I thought it was him coming back when I saw your lights—that's why I got excited and ran in front of your car. Virgil thinks it's wicked for me to go walking about like this, but Virgil thinks so many things are wicked. I wonder if that isn't the most sinful thing of all—thinking all the pleasant things are wicked."

Ada was talking to herself by this time. Danny could hear her voice getting fainter and fainter in the distance and there was no reply when Trace called out, "Can't we take you home?" Leave it to Trace to invite a passenger at a time like this! For a moment there was no sound at all except a mockingbird singing in the cemetery.

"That settles it!" Arthur announced, kicking the jeep into motion. "The farm is out! If that buzzy dame tells Virgil she saw us on the road—"

"She'll get herself into a peck of trouble," Trace finished.

But Trace didn't put up an argument when Arthur held his ground. The farm was risky. Ada Keep wasn't noted for her discretion; she might easily blurt out the story without realizing what she was saying. And she might even have caught a glimpse of Danny crouched in that back seat, a glimpse to be remembered when the mockingbirds were through singing.

So they took Danny to their crude little farmhouse at the edge of town, fed him eggs and coffee and thick slabs of bacon, and then made up a bundle of food and blankets. The last moonlight was fading when the jeep took to the road again. There was a deserted cabin at a place called Peace Canyon, and so long as it had a bed in it, Danny was satisfied.

Chapter Eleven

Trace was up early in the morning. The day was going to be difficult enough without the added worry of Danny's safety, a worry not a little agitated by the uncertainty of what Ada Keep might have told her husband. There was only one way to set his mind at ease on that score, and only one way to seek out an answer to a new question that had been bothering him since that midnight ride. Both ways led straight to Virgil's office.

As could be expected, Virgil was not in good humor. "I knew I should have stayed in bed," he muttered, at the sight of Trace coming through the doorway. "Didn't you cause me enough trouble yesterday without coming back for more?"

"Trouble?" Trace echoed innocently. "What did I do?"

"What did you do? In the first place, you got me to take that kid out to Mountain View. That wasn't so bad because there was me and a couple of my men to keep an eye on him, but then you had to insist on that wild-goose chase up to Raney's mine!"

"It wasn't a wild-goose chase. We learned there was a man in a raincoat."

"Was is right! Was is just right!"

Ada came in with a pot of coffee just then, but Virgil didn't so much as acknowledge her presence. The pressure must be getting pretty rough, Trace reckoned, because the big man's blustering manner had a graveness in it and lacked its usual steam even when he pushed back from the desk and began pacing the floor like an angry bull.

"Do you know what your precious Danny Ross has done now?" he stormed. "That man in the raincoat, Steve Malone, was found in Junction City last night with a bullet in his head. And who do you think was seen in Junction City last night? Who do you think held a gun—my gun—on a man parked at a drive-in, and then slugged him so he could follow Malone?"

"Was Malone shot with your gun?" Trace asked.

He shouldn't have been so casual about it. He should have shown some surprise, because Virgil calmed down right away.

"We don't know yet," he said.

"Then you don't know that Danny shot him."

"Well, what does it look like?"

"It looks," Trace murmured, helping himself to the coffee Virgil still ignored, "like three murders in a row. First Francy, then Doctor Gaynor, and now Malone. It looks like somebody trying desperately to silence anyone who might know the truth. That's the trouble with murder. It multiplies."

"Was Francy really murdered?" Ada asked.

It was easy to forget about Ada. She blended with the walls and the woodwork. Trace watched her over the rim of the coffee cup, trying to decide if she'd said anything about meeting him last night. He guessed not since Virgil had made no mention of it.

"Are you still here?" Virgil howled, giving her a push toward the hall. "I've told you a thousand times to keep your nose out of this office!" He returned to his desk and gave back the frown Trace had sent him. "You can't trust a woman," he muttered. "They pick up a little here, a little there, and then they go buzzing all over town until everybody's up in arms and ready to throw a necktie party at the first tree they come to. You may not know it, Trace, but that kid would be a lot safer in this jail than wherever he is now."

It could have been just conscience that made Virgil's words sound so deliberate. "I'll tell him if I see him," Trace muttered.

"You be sure and do that. And tell Laurent, too."

It definitely wasn't conscience, and this time Trace was caught way off base. "Laurent?" he echoed.

"Don't act innocent, Trace, it's not your type. Yes, I know all about Alexander Laurent coming into town night before last and having that heart-to-heart talk with you at the Pioneer bar. Of course, I'm not a smart, educated man like you two, but even a dumb sheriff knows a little of what happens in his own town." Virgil smiled, and he looked much less ominous without it. "The people on the street know about it too," he added, "and if they should get the idea that a great lawyer like Laurent was going to get Danny Ross out of paying for old Charley's death—"

"Only if he's innocent!" Trace cut in.

"You'll have to prove that."

"That's what I'm trying to do! I know the heat's all on you, Virgil, for letting Danny get away. But use your head. If it turns out he's just an innocent, scared kid, running the way any innocent, scared kid might run, then the last laugh is yours. But if you follow the mob and spend so much time looking for Danny you can't find the real murderer then you're not fit to be wearing that badge!"

Anyone but a Cooper would have caught a fist in his face for saying that. Virgil's face was white with fury. "Maybe you could wear it better!" he snapped.

"Maybe I could. Maybe I'd start by finding out something about Danny Ross—where he's from, what kind of a family, if he has a record. Just because he's a stranger doesn't make him a killer. And then I'd want to know what possible motive he could have had for doing these things. If he killed the old man for his money, why did he kill Malone?"

"Malone could have been a witness."

"To an act of Danny's? That doesn't make sense, Virgil. You wouldn't have known a thing about Malone if Danny hadn't insisted there was such a man. Why would he start a search for a man who could convict him? And while we're on the subject of Malone, how was he fixed for folding money when they found him?"

It hit home. Virgil knew as well as Trace that a common laborer at Raney's camp didn't drag down that kind of money, plus room and board, for a couple of weeks work.

Besides, Malone had left a trail of twenty-dollar bills all over Junction City. But Virgil wasn't cowed for long.

"Get the kid back here and I'll try to get some answers for those questions," he said. "I can't examine a suspect when he's not on hand."

"You can check his background."

"Hell, man, he wouldn't give us any!" Virgil ripped open one of the lower desk drawers and brought up a canvas zipper bag, a paper-covered book, and a well-worn wallet. "That's all he had on him," he said. "Some underwear and socks, this darned book, and the two hundred dollars."

"No identification?"

"The usual. Driver's license, social security—"

"Then he had been working."

"Why not? He's old enough. Over eighteen."

"Over eighteen?" Trace picked up the wallet and studied the driver's license inside. Chicago, the address was. Just as he expected. It was a couple of years old so the address might be out of date, but it would be all right for a starter. The snapshots were cute but uninformative, and there was nothing to indicate Danny Ross was anything but what he claimed to be: a kid on the loose seeing the country. Nothing except what was missing. Trace was on the verge of mentioning it when he caught himself. Danny was in enough trouble already without stirring up more, and he might be jumping to conclusions anyway. It was just that the kid had been so reluctant to give himself a past—and so eager to leave a murder charge hanging over him by skipping over the border. Trace fingered the language dictionary thoughtfully.

"Like I said before," Virgil remarked, "we'll get all kinds of answers when Danny's back in that cell, but until then my one and only interest is finding him before some not so law-abiding citizens do. Right now I'm going to pay a call on your friend Laurent."

"Do you think he's keeping the kid?"

"I don't know. All I know is that one of the boys reported seeing headlights moving out that way late last night, and they've combed all over Junction City."

Trace still had the feeling that Virgil wasn't telling him all these things just to make conversation. The headlights could have been the jeep hurrying off to Peace Canyon, and Virgil's proclaimed visit to the ranch could be a ruse to send him out after Danny so he could be followed. If so Virgil was out of luck, because now Trace had to go to a funeral.

Two funerals were held that morning in the little frame church adjoining the Cooperton cemetery. This unusually crowded calendar brought great mental anguish to the man in charge of operations, particularly in the instance of the woman named Francy Allen. The Reverend Mr. Whitlow, a placid man of sufficient years to make such a condition possible, had no objection to performing such services for a sinner. As a matter of fact, it was his private opinion that such as Francy needed his prayers far more than the good Doctor Gaynor; but his discomfort at the thought of these two more or less consecutive ceremonies concerned not the dead but the living. It was common knowledge that Francy Allen had come between Trace Cooper and Joyce Gaynor, and so solemn an occasion was hardly the time to renew old bitterness.

Francy's funeral was brief and her mourners few. The entire party consisted of four members: Trace, looking strangely dignified in a dark suit specially pressed for the occasion—no doubt about it, the Coopers were a striking breed even in decline; an individual named Murphy, who carried on the dubious profession of tending bar at the Pioneer Hotel and who insisted on crossing himself at prayer; Fisher the mortician, and Trace's dark companion whose presence in the Cooperton church and cemetery might be tolerated in life but never in death. This situation was not particularly to the Reverend Mr. Whitlow's liking, but it was not without experience that he had become a placid man.

The last amen was uttered with a profound sense of gratitude that there had been no overlapping of mourners. The trouble between Trace and Joyce Gaynor seemed to worsen with the passing of time. It was, Reverend Mr. Whitlow reckoned, due in great part to the attentions paid her by the young doctor who had come to carry on a practice death would have ended in due time at any rate. It was none of the Reverend's business, of course, but he did hate to see a courtship of such long standing fail. Trace and Joyce had been going out together even before he went into the service. Adjustments had to be made later, particularly in view of Trace's loss of the ranch, but Joyce wasn't one to let money or the lack of it come between her and the man she loved. But Francy was a different matter. If only Trace hadn't taken her under his roof—with the whole town knowing what she was!

The last amen and the scraping of spades on the dry earth. Murph and Arthur left the churchyard, and Fisher hurried off to attend to the new procession already creeping up the road, but Trace stayed on. He knew exactly what the minister was thinking; he knew exactly how the town would buzz if he remained for the doctor's funeral. It was a ridiculous situation. Old Doc Gaynor had brought him into the world and watched over him for years like a benevolent grandfather, but because of one quarrel, one misunderstanding, and all the heartaches that went with it, he was now an outsider.

Trace watched them come—the hearse, the black limousine, and just about every vehicle of transportation in the county following behind. All of Cooperton, it appeared, would be at Charley Gaynor's funeral, not to mention representatives of all the outlying areas that had known his friendly smile and merciful hands. A good man dies poor but with many mourners, and none of the Coopers sleeping under their ornate stone angels had inspired such a cortege as this! Reluctantly, Trace moved off toward where Arthur waited in the jeep. Absence was the best way to pay his respects; what's more, the sight of that long, crawling train had given him an idea. What better time to do a few of the things that must be done than when so many of the cats were away?

And so the Reverend Mr. Whitlow drew a sigh of heartfelt relief, and all the Coopertonians were cheated of an anticipated scene that could in no way approach the scandalous behavior of Trace Cooper's next move.

. . . The first move was to send Arthur off on the bus to Red Rock. From there he could send a telegram that wouldn't immediately become public property, as well as make a few inquiries at the hospital where Francy had died.

Trace didn't know exactly what to look for, but he was beginning to get an idea. All of this meant delaying the report to Laurent until sometime later in the afternoon, but with Virgil already at the ranch it was wiser to stay away for a while anyway. The time wouldn't be wasted.

Nobody locked doors in Cooperton. The bank, the gas pumps, a few houses of business—yes; but not the tall, old-fashioned doors of the houses where people lived and died. Doctor Gaynor's house was no different from the others. A sad-eyed collie guarded the wide front porch, his long muzzle sunk deep within his paws, but he was an old dog and Trace was an old friend of the master who wouldn't return. A few words of comfort, a pat on the head, and the responding slap of a shaggy tail on the plank step comprised the only formalities to this entrance.

Inside the house all was silent and heavy with the perfume of death, of wreaths and bouquets that had stopped by on the way to the churchyard and become mingled with the faintly medicinal odor of the doctor's home office. Trace slid open the double doors and stepped into the dispensary. White and clean were the walls, black and shiny were the leather swivel chair and the rolled-top desk. Where did the search begin? Where was the evidence that might spell murder if seen by understanding eyes? Trace moved over to the desk.

A doctor's life was a life of confidences, sometimes freely, sometimes reluctantly given, and his records were meant for his eyes alone. Trace knew these things but he had to go on prodding every pigeonhole and rifling every drawer. The fat-faced clock hung over a glass-front cabinet with locked doors ticked off a steady warning, but the search continued. Old records, old secrets, old X rays—these were no good! What was needed was something recent, some starting place for murder such as the day before Francy died. There must be an appointment book somewhere. . . .

Trace was reaching for yet another drawer when noises on the front porch brought a sudden halt to his activities. So soon? He swung about and looked at the fat clock, and was astonished at the time. The funeral must be over. The noises were footsteps and voices on the porch.

"I don't like leaving you alone at a time like this," the

young doctor was saying as the front door opened. "I'd be only too glad to stay."

"No, Lowell, please—I don't mind. I'd rather be alone."

Just hearing Joyce speak again brought a tightness to Trace's throat. He moved away from the doorway and stood pressed against the wall.

"Well, if you're sure you don't mind. But if you need anything, don't hesitate to call."

Need anything! As if Joyce Gaynor had to rely on Lowell Glenn for her needs! Trace waited for the click of the closing door, and then for the sound of Joyce coming nearer. She came slowly and at last stood in the double doorway, her face terribly young and terribly solemn under a small black hat. He could see she was troubled by the opened doors until the sight of him gave her bigger troubles.

"Trace," she gasped, "what are you doing here? What have you done to grandfather's things?"

It was too late for discretion. He'd had neither time nor thought for closing the desk. "I'm looking for something," he said.

"I can see that, but what are you looking for?"

"I'm not sure. A beginning, a reason for three violent deaths."

These first few moments were the most difficult—this first shock of finding him here in the house; but if Trace won these moments, he might win time to finish the search. Joyce hesitated and then came into the room.

"You're trying to help Danny Ross," she said. "Why?"

"Because he's innocent."

"How can you be sure?"

There was a strangeness in her voice that made Trace uncomfortable. "I'm not sure," he answered, "but I'm not the only one who feels this way. Alexander Laurent was the first. He asked me to defend Danny."

"In court?"

"We hope it doesn't go that far."

Joyce was impressed. She knew what the name Laurent stood for in the pursuit of justice, and what it meant to Trace. No one could have known Trace so long and so well without knowing his idols. Her hesitation was a green light for the full treatment.

"Can't you see?" Trace argued. "Your grandfather had no enemies; he could only have been killed because something he knew or suspected was dangerous to someone. And what could he have known? Think, Joyce. It was he who answered the call when Francy was found dying on the highway. He gave her emergency treatment, and was with her in the hospital when she died. And on his way home to make an official report on the cause of her death he was killed. Everybody loved Charley Gaynor, but it seems to me that somebody loved life a lot more."

"But the money—" she protested.

"Haven't you heard about Danny's man in a raincoat? He was found in Junction City last night with a bullet in his head and quite a stack of twenty-dollar bills in his possession."

Joyce was trying hard to keep up with his arguments, he had to give her credit for that, but the ordeal she'd just been through made it all so difficult. Death, that's all she could retain. Sudden, horrible, violent death. Black wasn't her color and cold-blooded logic wasn't her forte.

"I'm sorry about Francy," she said vaguely. "I meant to send flowers but there was so much to do."

"It doesn't matter," Trace muttered. "She couldn't have smelled them anyway. Joyce, I'm not doing this because of Francy. I'm here for the living, not the dead!"

He wanted to say so much more, but they mustn't get started talking about Francy. Francy always led to an impasse, and at the moment all he wanted to lead to was that appointment book. It took a bit of doing, but in the end Joyce agreed, and they studied it together. The last page was filled with dates that would never be kept, but it was the day of Francy's death that interested Trace. What he expected to find was vague and nebulous in his mind, and what he did find did nothing to better that condition. The doctor had put in a routine day. A local hypochondriac, a couple of regular visits from expectant mothers, and only one patient who elicited any interest at all.

"Ada Keep," Trace wondered aloud. "What's troubling Ada? Surely she isn't in a family way!"

Joyce almost smiled. "Poor Ada," she murmured. "I don't know what she came to Grandfather for—sympathy perhaps. I think he was running some kind of tests."

"I.Q.?"

"You shouldn't talk that way!"

"I know." Trace slammed the book shut with a gesture of finality. It had seemed such a good idea, too. But at least the morning hadn't been wasted. He had been with Joyce all this time without argument, and even now, when there was no excuse left for staying, she hadn't asked him to leave. Perhaps it was because death in the house brought back mutual memories, and not all of them were bad. Not nearly all.

"Joyce," he began, knowing in his heart it was useless effort. Automatically she drew away and became terribly preoccupied straightening the old man's desk, much as if he'd be coming back soon and might scold if things were out of place. The appointment book went back into the top drawer, the letters back into the pigeonholes, and an old fountain pen left uncapped required immediate attention. "This old pen!" she fussed, screwing on the top fiercely. "With all the fine pens Grandfather's been given, he always uses some leaky old thing like this!"

Just a cheap fountain pen, but through it came all the meaning of death. Joyce slumped down in the old leather chair and began to cry softly while the pen twisted foolishly between her fingers. "Joyce, honey—" Trace's arm was about her shaking shoulders in an instant, but the impulse was a very bad guess. "Leave me alone!" she cried. "Get out of here! It's all your fault!"

"My fault? Good lord, Joyce, what are you saying?"

"You and Francy! If my grandfather was murdered because of Francy Allen it's your fault. You brought her back here!"

"Of course I did. She was half dead when that butcher in Red Rock got through with her. What else could I do?"

"You could have married her!"

It took a moment such as this to break through the wall of ice and reach the core of her anger. Now that it was said there were no words left between them. Trace turned on his heel and left the house as silently as he'd come, and was blocks away before he remembered what was on Joyce's hand where she held the pen. A blue stain, a smudge just like the one the mortician had found on Francy's fingers.

Chapter Twelve

Peace Canyon was a world without sound. There were no trees for the winds to rustle (and seldom any wind), no highways bustling with traffic, and no living things except the little ground creatures that crawled or scampered between the rocks. The cabin to which Trace had taken Danny stood on a clearing on the canyon floor, sheltered and lonely and so weathered by time that it blended with the crusty soil like some native growth. There were two buildings actually—the cabin and a small barn, and since they were built close to the east wall of the canyon the sun was a long time reaching them.

It was the sun that awakened Danny. It must have been noon or after from the heat of it, and the cabin had become an oven while he slept. He came out of a troubled dream sweating and peeled off the leather jacket he'd been wearing all this time. Exhaustion and caution had prevented taking stock of this sanctuary earlier—lighting the lamp he'd found on the table seemed unwise—but now he could sit on the edge of the bunk and survey the entire cabin. It consisted of just one small room with a black kerosene stove and a cupboard at one end, the table and a couple of chairs in between, and an old-fashioned dresser at the far wall. It looked like an overnight stopping place for a range rider, or maybe just a place to hole in if a fellow got fed up with people. For Danny it was just fine, and then he became aware of an uncomfortable sensation that, on closer analysis, turned out to be hunger.

The food Trace had left him was in a cardboard box on the table: a few tins, some cheese, and a canteen of water. The cheese and the water were all right, but the tins weren't much good without a can opener, and Danny's pockets were clean after being relieved of his possessions by the sheriff. According to Trace the cabin hadn't been used for years, but since the furnishings were intact there was a chance a few utensils might be left in that cupboard. It was worth a look.

The very first door he tried brought a surprise. No can opener but something a lot more interesting—beer. Half a dozen cans of beer as well as a bottle of bourbon about two-thirds empty. Maybe this was a thoughtful gesture left for any wayfaring stranger, but if so the wayfarers must have been regular customers because there was no dust on the cans and no dust on the neck of the bottle. Now Danny forgot about the can opener. He ripped open the other cupboards and took stock of the contents: a couple of glasses, a few pieces of cheap china, a can of coffee, and a small slab of unsliced bacon. Even a loaf of bread that didn't feel stale to the touch! Of course he'd heard stories, some of them pretty tall, about how long food remained fresh in the desert air, but this stuff, was a little too fresh for comfort.

A quick look about the room affirmed his fear. This cabin hadn't sat empty all these years since Trace sold the ranch; it had been occupied and not very long ago. The lamp on the table was filled with kerosene, the wavy mirror over the dresser was free of dust and grime, and a cracked saucer on the dresser top was filled with cigarette butts of a recent vintage. What made the butts so interesting were the lipstick stains on some of them. No cowboy or bindle stiff had left those! And then Danny looked down at his feet and spied another stain even more interesting.

The curse of blood seemed to be following Danny Ross: first the old doctor's blood that somehow got all over his hands and face, then the blood coming from that little hole in Steve Malone's forehead, and now a wide brown stain on the bare floor boards beneath his feet. He didn't have a doubt in the world but what it was blood. It figured, didn't it? Everywhere he went was grief.

This had been a big grief. The first wide stain was only the beginning; beyond it he found the little stains like drops making a trail across the floor. It was an easy trail to follow once he'd found it, and it led straight to the door. Outside was a little flat roofed porch and the stains were there, too, but where they led farther was something he could not know. The floor of the canyon was a moving thing constantly shifting and sifting so that footprints or bloodstains were lost almost as soon as they were made. But from the porch Danny's eye traveled naturally to the barn a few yards to the rear.

He didn't want to go into the barn. He didn't want to stumble across another corpse, but by this time he couldn't help himself. Already his imagination was building up another crime of violence, for it was a cinch all that blood hadn't come from a cut finger. . . . The double doors opened easily, and for a few moments he was blinded by the sudden darkness after all that sunlight. Then the sunlight began to creep in from a hundred cracks in the siding and the roof, and to pour in from that opened door. . . . Danny breathed easier. This time his luck had changed. This time no corpse.

No corpse, no blood, no gory weapon . . . "Kid, you're getting jumpy," he said aloud, and the sound of his own voice was like that of a stranger.

But that still left a brown stain on the cabin floor. He looked in the stalls—a long time empty from the looks of them—and even raised the lid on a feed bin that held nothing but about a handful of oats. No four-footed animal had left any recent trace, but the soft earthen floor showed a perfect set of tire prints—heavy-duty treads that might have come from a truck or a jeep.

Danny squatted on his heels in the dust and tried to make something of a combination like bloodstains in the cabin and tire marks in the barn, and after what he'd been through these past few days there was no limit to what could be made of it. But all the time the canyon was as peaceful as its name, and the sun beat down with warm reassurance. Broad daylight was no time for nightmares. Trace Cooper would come around in a few hours and explain the whole thing; meantime, he was supposed to stay under cover instead of going about looking for more trouble. With a whistle on his lips, forced and not too effective, Danny retraced his steps to the cabin and opened the door. It was too late then to do anything about the uninvited guest waiting for him inside. . . .

It was a man Danny had never seen before. It was a man who looked like a boy at first sight and grew older before his eyes. He was slender and tall, with a fine high forehead crowned by a crest of blond waves, and an expression of startled bewilderment on his patrician face that was a perfect match for Danny's sentiments. He stood beside the bunk holding Danny's leather jacket in one hand and the sheriff's revolver in the other.

"What are you doing here?" he demanded. "What are you doing in my cabin?"

The question made no more sense than the man's presence. Danny took the cabin to be Trace's.

"That's my business," he said.

"Your business? Did you ask my permission? Does anybody ever ask my permission?" The jacket was hurled to the floor in an angry gesture, but he wasn't letting go of that gun. It looked ridiculous dangling from his long white hand. He was white all over, this man. White skin, whitish hair, white flannel trousers—like a refugee from a tennis court or a musical comedy chorus.

"I know what you come here for!" he blazed. "I won't have my cabin used for that sort of thing! I won't have that woman coming here any more!"

Danny wanted to duck and run, but he also wanted to know what was ailing this guy. "What woman?" he asked.

"That terrible woman! She comes here all the time with her men friends. She leaves the place in a terrible mess. Look for yourself—"

"It looks all right to me," Danny said.

"Oh, it does!" With his free hand the man reached over and ripped open the top dresser drawer. It was filled with a most amazing collection of articles for a rancher's outpost cabin: a sheer nightgown, a negligee, a full array of feminine finery sticky with the scent of cheap perfume. "Her things, all her smelly things," the man shouted. "Her things in every drawer!"

He seemed almost to have forgotten Danny, busy as he was scooping the unwanted articles from the dresser drawer by drawer. A filmy handkerchief landed at Danny's feet and he stooped to pick it up. It was a cheap lace affair with a huge monogram of one letter: F.

"Francy!" Danny said.

"Then you do know her!"

"No. No I don't. I only heard of her."

As mad as this guy was, Danny wanted no part of Francy Allen. In fact, he no longer wanted the cabin. "I came here alone," he added. "I'm not staying. I'll get out right now. . . ."

Very gladly would he get out right now! Apparently this indignant owner didn't read the papers or listen to the radio, because up to now he'd shown no interest in Danny's identity. He was just a trespasser on private property.

"Wait a minute!"

So long as he held that gun anything the man said was an order. Danny waited.

"Get this stuff out of here!"

"But it's not mine!"

"I don't care whose it is; get it out!"

Danny had his arms full of some pretty silly articles when the man in white jerked open the bottom drawer. It stuck at first and then let go all the way, spilling both drawer and contents at his feet. Suddenly Danny was looking at a brown stain again, and this time there was no doubt about what it was. It was a black iron skillet with some blond hairs matted and stuck on the bottom, and it was a towel that had been white before it absorbed all that blood.

Gun or no gun, Danny wasn't sticking around to be blamed for this too. He let fly with the lingerie and was halfway across the barnyard before the shot came.

Chapter Thirteen

Danny ran. He heard the shot but didn't look back; every second counted now. The road was behind him—he couldn't take that way out—but once he'd reached the far side of the barn he was at least out of the line of fire. Beyond the barn the east wall of the canyon stretched like a crooked corrugated fence, jutting out here, cutting in there, and providing plenty of boulders and ravines to use as a hiding place. But there was no hiding place from the sun.

The canyon floor was as hot as the basement of hell, but Danny kept on running. Who that excitable man back at the cabin might be didn't concern him at the moment. He had the gun, Danny's erstwhile comforter, and in another man's hand it wasn't at all comforting. And what was the man to think walking in on a trespasser, a gun, and the ugly evidence in that bottom drawer? The chain of circumstance was getting heavier and heavier; Danny could actually feel the drag of it, and his steps began to falter until the run became a walk and the walk became a senseless stumbling.

When the dust came up and hit him in the face, Danny rested. He listened for pursuing footsteps, but the only sound was the heavy pounding of his own heart. From his knees he turned and looked back. No sign of the cabin now. Only silence and emptiness and that terrible white fire in the sky. A man with a gun in his hand could never be such an enemy as that sun.

"Mr. Cooper!" Danny yelled. "Mr. Cooper!"

Then he clapped a hand over his mouth. It was a crazy waste of precious strength to be yelling that way. Trace Cooper wasn't in the canyon now, and when he did return, he'd find nothing but an empty cabin. Danny could never make it back even if he knew the way.

When Trace remembered the blue smudge on Francy's dead fingers, he went immediately to Fisher's Mortuary. It was a routine trip; he knew without asking that the smudge was an inkstain, and that was an interesting fact, considering whose hand it was on. Fisher concurred readily.

"It was ink," he said. "Messy stuff to get off. I had the same trouble with Charley Gaynor."

"Charley too?" Trace echoed. "Was there ink on Charley's fingers?"

"That's right, the same as Francy. Say, you know that's peculiar."

Trace didn't need Fisher to tell him that. The sight of Virgil's borrowed transportation returning to Main Street told him the coast was clear for reporting to Laurent, but he had to pass the Pioneer Hotel on the way back and the bar was open by this time. Maybe Murph could shed some light on the mystery.

Funerals made Murph thirsty. He was opening himself another bottle of beer when Trace came in, and it was only natural to suppose he'd come with a similar desire. But this time it was no sale. Murph looked hurt. "What are you trying to do," he muttered, "put me out of business?"

"I'm in a hurry," Trace said. "I just want to ask a few questions."

A very few questions. The whereabouts of Francy Allen on the night before her death; the company she kept, the things she said and did.

"Are you kidding?" Murph asked. "No, guess you ain't. I guess you weren't in much shape to remember."

"Remember what?"

"You and Francy right here at this bar fighting like a couple of banty roosters. I usually don't listen in, but you were trying to get her to come back to the farm, and she was telling you to mind your own business, or something like that. Finally she went into the dining room and sat at the table with Jim Rice and some cattleman he was entertaining."

Trace tried to remember. He knew he'd had trouble with Francy, nothing but trouble for a long time, but when he got to drinking heavy, things had a way of blacking out.

"What did I do?" he asked.

"After I called Arthur, you went home like a good boy. At least you went out of here. Christ, Trace, but you get mean when you're loaded!"

"And what did Francy do?"

Murph finished off the beer in one long, satisfying attack, wiped off his moist mouth, and grinned. "I never kept tabs on Francy," he said. "That would have taken a considerable chunk out of my life."

"You didn't see her writing anything? You didn't notice her using a pen?"

"Using a pen?" The way Murph looked he must have figured Trace had been out in the sun too long. "Hell," he muttered, reaching for another beer, "I didn't even know Francy could write!"

In his crude way Murph had summed up the situation thoroughly. Francy probably hadn't written a letter since Trace came back from overseas, and she didn't have a bank account to draw on or a phone number to write down for a visiting cattleman. The odds were against her using a pen at all that night, yet sometime during the night she'd been slugged or hit by a truck and left dying on the highway—only to turn up at the mortuary the next day with inkstains on her fingers. Murph wouldn't have known the answer to that puzzler if Trace had asked him, but some of the answers Arthur might bring back from Red Rock could prove interesting. Until then there was still a little matter of consulting with Alexander Laurent. . . .

For the second time in five years Trace went home again. He might as well admit it; that's what the ranch would always mean—home, with a memory in every mile of the road, in every bend and every dry wash. The same lean-faced ranch hands occupied the bunkhouse, the same dark-skinned servants padded quietly in and out the kitchen; and in the high-ceilinged living room, with its thick walls exiling the sun, the oil portrait of an ancestor with Trace Cooper's face stared down coldly from above the mantle. With the exception of a grand piano standing where the spinet of Grandmother Trace had stood, the room was just as it had been in its glory. But a stranger sat in the master's chair.

At least the stranger was gracious. A hot ride in an open jeep called for an iced drink before conversation, and not until Ramón had filled the master's request could there be any exchange of confidences. Trace had a pair of inkstains on his mind, but Laurent had the sheriff's visit.

"Of course I heard of the boy's escape yesterday on the radio," he said, "but I never dreamed the sheriff would connect that with me. What did you tell him about our conversation?"

"Not a thing," Trace answered. "Cooperton has a lot of ears—all big."

"I suppose so, but it's regrettable—the boy's escape, I mean. If he should be caught trying to cross the border—"

"He won't be," Trace promised.

"Then you know where he is?"

"I do. Danny and I had an unscheduled meeting last night in the room of a brand-new corpse named Steve Malone."

Laurent's glass didn't quite reach his lips. He'd heard of Malone's death, of course, from Virgil; but that slight frown creasing his high forehead betrayed a trace of surprise.

"Danny didn't kill Malone," Trace added.

"Are you quite sure of that?"

"Quite sure, and for two reasons. In the first place, that gun Danny took off the sheriff hasn't been fired; I know because it was waving under my nose most of the time we were in that room. In the second place, why should Danny kill his alibi? A dead Malone can't back up his story of what happened to the doctor's missing wallet."

"The wallet—" The way Laurent quietly froze in his chair was silent testimony to his accelerated interest. "Have you found the wallet?"

It was an anticlimax to be forced to answer in the negative. Trace explained about the bank roll on Malone's bed and the trail of ready cash he'd followed to that hotel; but Malone without the wallet didn't prove a thing. He might have picked up that extra windfall in a crap game or rolled someone even drunker than himself. He might have collected an old debt, or any number of other absurdities that any first-rate prosecutor intent on hanging Danny Ross would not hesitate to point out. Laurent listened politely, but his mind was already racing on to other things.

"It's no matter," he said, brushing aside the argument with a dismissing hand. "I've been thinking things over, and it seems to me now that the wallet is irrelevant. As a matter of fact, so is the late Mr. Malone."

"The police don't share your view," Trace remarked.

"Oh, a murder is a murder; I'm not forgetting Malone. It's just that whatever he could have contributed to clearing up this affair died with him. Now we must look elsewhere. Now we must look for the roots. And the roots, Mr. Cooper, may go very deep. . . . You were, I believe, a close friend of the good doctor's last patient."

It was Trace's turn to freeze in position now. He'd been thinking of Francy all morning, but he'd never expected to have Alexander Laurent bring her into the conversation. And certainly not in so pointed a way! "For a recluse you seem amazingly well up on the local gossip," he observed. "It's not too difficult to see where you got it, with Charley Gaynor coming out here so often."

"The servants—" Laurent began, but Trace would have none of that.

"No, not the servants," he insisted. "I know these people, Mr. Laurent. They chatter among themselves as much as you and I, but they're choosy about sharing a confidence. I just can't see Ramón, for instance, coming to you with the latest scandal. If we must discuss my relationship with Francy Allen let's at least start with the truth."

Laurent smiled and nodded his approval. "Sound reasoning," he said. "That comes in handy in a courtroom. . . . Yes, it was Doctor Gaynor who told me about Miss Allen, but in all fairness I must admit to leading him on. It was some months ago—time means little to me any more—when we were playing chess of an evening. The doctor seemed quite unlike himself: distraught, troubled, unable to concentrate. Since conversation is the best antidote for worry, I drew him out. Little by little he told me the whole story."

"He couldn't have told you the whole story," Trace snapped. "He never knew the whole story."

"That's quite possible. The whole story is rarely known by any one individual, but there's no reason to doubt that he did know the principals of this one. One he had brought into the world, the other was his own granddaughter, and the third—"

"Was a human being!"

"Too much so! It was a rather sad story, as I recall, concerning a young woman who went bad and a promising young man who seemed to prefer her to his fiancée. Temporarily at least."

"That's a lie!" Trace exclaimed. "I took Francy into my home because she was in trouble and had no place to go. Even an animal is entitled to decent care at a time like that."

"And prior to the trouble?"

Trace was going to get good and mad pretty soon, and not with Laurent but with himself. He'd come here to discuss Danny Ross and a mess called murder—not the private life of Francy Allen! And he didn't have to go on with it, but he would. Something about that calm expectancy of Alexander Laurent made it perfectly plain that he would. No wonder the man was a master at cross-examination!

"You don't understand about Francy," he said. "Nobody does. She grew up on this ranch. She belonged here. She was a part of something solid and secure that was going to last forever, and she didn't have to worry about a thing."

Trace couldn't sit there any longer with his grandfather's face staring down at him. He got up and stood with his back to the cold mantel.

"But it didn't last forever," he said bitterly. "It fell into the hands of a crazy fool who couldn't recognize ruin when it was all about him. He went overseas to find something easier to fight than himself, but Francy didn't have any place to run. She stayed and went down with the wreckage."

"And you blame yourself," Laurent observed.

"Who else is to blame?"

It was good to have it said at last. Now Trace could forgive Laurent's prying; what's more, the man seemed to understand. Without knowing Francy, without remembering her through a score of years, Alexander Laurent accepted without question what Trace supposed no one could comprehend.

"*Noblesse oblige*," he murmured. "One does find it in unexpected places. Not that your attitude surprises me, Mr. Cooper. I've seen you with your other adopted burden— your partner, I believe you call him."

"Arthur is my partner!"

"Of course he is, but where do you suppose he would be without your protection? Oh, I'm not scolding. Every man's entitled to choose his own cross, but it does seem that you've gone rather far afield."

"Maybe we'd better get back to the subject at hand," Trace suggested, but Laurent smiled knowingly.

"We've never left it," he said. "Since you indicate, and I believe you, that Doctor Gaynor erred in fixing the blame for the illegal operation he was called upon to mend, an interesting thought arises. Who was responsible?"

It wasn't the first time Trace had faced that question. Francy was a stranger to him after he came home from the war: a wild, careless creature with her laughter too loud and her thirst too long. She seemed determined on self-destruction, and her affairs were her affairs . . . affairs without names. But Laurent was waiting for his answer.

"I don't know," Trace said. "Francy never told me and I never asked."

"Noble," Laurent conceded, "but hardly practical. Now if you had asked—"

"Don't you suppose anyone did? Charley Gaynor, for instance. When she wouldn't answer, he took it for granted that she was shielding me. Francy was loyal in her way."

"A rather peculiar way! She must have known what her silence would cost you."

"Why? Francy wasn't the kind to walk out on a man because of some dirty gossip!"

Trace swung about and stared into the black mouth of the fireplace. He was saying too much; he was letting too much show, and this man's eyes and ears were the collection agencies for a most discerning mind. "Nevertheless," he was saying, "it would be extremely helpful to know that man. Suppose, for example, he made promises he couldn't keep . . . or threats that he could. Surely you must realize by this time that our trail leads back to Miss Allen. There can be no other reason for the doctor's death than what he must have known about this man."

It was an oversimplification, but when Laurent spoke, it became the judgment of Jehovah. And Trace would be starting from scratch. Francy had stayed at the farm spasmodically. It was on again, off again, between jobs in town —usually at the Pioneer Hotel until the lady vigilantes had Virgil speak to the management. At the hotel she met everybody from the locals who patronized the bar to every visiting salesman, mining engineer, and cattle buyer. . . . Trace raised his head. Maybe it was just an association of ideas, but suddenly he had a longing to have a talk with Jim Rice. Jim always had an eye for the ladies; he couldn't have overlooked Francy.

"A promise, a threat, or an attachment," Laurent added thoughtfully. "Some such thing must have kept Miss Allen silent . . . and some such thing must have come to the doctor's attention."

The door was wide open for Trace to lead into the subject of the inkstained fingers, but the door to the patio was also open, and this was the door that arrested his attention as he turned around. A man was coming across the patio at an unsteady gait—half run, half stumble. He made straight for the house and burst into the living room with no more ceremony than a barbarian descending upon Rome.

"Why, Douglas!" Laurent gasped, coming to his feet. "What's happened? What have you done?"

It was more than the sudden and unexpected entry that prompted this anxiety. Douglas Laurent was in a state of disheveled agitation. His nice white trousers were streaked with dirt and his expensive sport shirt looked as if he'd been rolling in barbed wire. He stood framed in that bright doorway, blinded for the moment by the contrasting darkness, and then Laurent the elder was between him and Trace, a fatherly arm about the boyish shoulders and all of that cold unemotionalism gone out of his voice.

"You've been running," he scolded gently. "You know that you mustn't run, Douglas, especially not in the hot sun."

"I had to run," Douglas gasped. "The fire!"

"Of course it's like fire . . . and no hat either! You'll have to excuse us, Mr. Cooper, but my son's health isn't up to this sort of thing."

"What's that in his hand?" Trace demanded.

He couldn't see the hand in question at the moment, Laurent was in the way, but he'd seen it clear enough when Douglas came through that doorway. "His hand?" Laurent looked at Trace oddly, and then backed away. "Why," he said, "it's a gun!"

It was a gun all right, and a gun Trace wasn't likely to forget after the way Danny had been pointing it at him last night. "Where did you get this?" he demanded. "Where did you find it?"

By this time Douglas Laurent's eyes must be adjusted to the light of the room, and there surely wasn't anything wrong with his hearing. "The gun," Trace repeated loudly. "Where did you get Virgil Keep's gun?"

"Virgil's!" Douglas might be momentarily dumb, but his father had a tongue. "Do you mean this is the weapon Danny Ross took from the sheriff?"

"I'm sure of it. And Danny was hanging on to it like a drowning man clutching a life belt when I left him last night. Your son's health may be delicate, Mr. Laurent, but not nearly so delicate as Danny's may be if those trigger-happy deputies have stumbled onto that cabin in Peace Canyon!"

Trace had no idea how he'd been shouting until the silence came. Total, complete silence, and then Laurent's voice like a hollow echo.

"Is that where you left him . . . in that cabin?"

"Why not? Nobody's used it for years."

He didn't get an argument—not in words. He got a pair of undefinable stares, and then Douglas began to laugh softly. "Nobody," he said. "Nobody at all! Well, she won't use it any more. No one will ever use it now."

Trace didn't understand what he was hearing, but he'd heard enough to head him for the door. "Where are you going?" Laurent demanded. It was a foolish question. "I'm going to that cabin," Trace said. "I'm going to find out what this is all about!"

"You can't!"

The words came from Douglas, and Trace wasn't likely to take orders from the likes of him. "And why can't I?" he demanded. "Who's going to stop me?"

"The fire," Douglas said. "It's all burning down . . . the cabin and everything in it."

Chapter Fourteen

Fire. Douglas had used the word before. He'd tried to tell them about the fire and been silenced in the discussion of the gun. But this was no time for regrets. That dry shell of the cabin would go up like a matchbox and somewhere, in it or mercifully out of it, Danny was in danger.

"Did you see him?" Trace cried. "Did you see Danny Ross?"

"Douglas doesn't know anything about Danny Ross," Laurent said. "The name means nothing to him."

"It's been on the radio enough these past two days."

"Douglas never listens to the radio."

It was maddening to have him stand there like that, disheveled and dazed and with that telltale gun in his hand and not a word on his lips. Trace couldn't wait around for stumbling explanations. He left the elder Laurent to get to the bottom of Douglas' adventure and raced for the jeep in the driveway. From the road he could see a plume of white smoke lifting up from behind a yonder ridge like a beckoning finger, and he made for that plume with the accelerator flat against the floor boards.

Trace wasn't the sole observer of that smoke signal . . . and it was like a signal to all who saw it. There was little wind in Peace Canyon at such an hour of the day, and the white plume rose straight and high for all eyes to see. The valley was full of eyes that day. Failure to find Danny Ross in Junction City had turned the search back toward its source; for if Danny had one friend that friend was Trace Cooper, and Trace specialized in reckless acts. Hiding a fugitive of the law would probably come under the heading of exciting sport. So reasoned Virgil Keep when his morning visit to Laurent provided no more than an excursion rich in fluent conversation and destitute of consequence.

But where would Trace conceal a fugitive? The farm was too obvious, and a quick check on his way back to town took care of Virgil's curiosity in that direction. The place was deserted except for the usual quota of dogs in the barnyard. But the longer Virgil considered the matter the more sure he became that Trace must know something. He'd been entirely too calm about Malone's death this morning, just as if he'd known all about it before Virgil broke the news. Just as if he'd heard the whole story from a firsthand witness. Even Trace Cooper couldn't be that cool about a third violent death within forty-eight hours.

One, two, three. . . . They were beginning to add up, and so was the pressure on Virgil Keep. He studied that map on his office wall, but this time the question wasn't where Danny might be hiding . . . it was where he might be hidden. That old Cooper ranch was honeycombed with hiding places, caves, ravines, and old outbuildings that a man like Alexander Laurent would neither know nor care about; but Trace knew them all. And so Virgil went a hunting and found—hung like a chiffon scarf against the turquoise sky—a signpost of smoke.

The trail to Peace Canyon was corrugated with the wear and weather of many years, and Virgil wasn't driving the four-wheeled counterpart of a mountain goat. Even so he reached the cabin site ahead of Trace, and by then the building was a black ruin. Orange flames still licked at the smoldering uprights, but the roof had fallen, most of the walls were gone, and the galvanized sheeting over the heavy plank porch teetered crazily between the skeleton supports of the few posts the flames had so far spared. He crawled out of his car and surveyed the scene with a sense of futility and wonder. A deserted cabin couldn't set itself afire, but if any living thing had been in that inferno the ashes would have to be sifted to find the bones.

". . . Danny! Danny Ross!"

Virgil whirled about to meet the cry behind him. The wheels of the jeep had hardly stopped turning before Trace was racing toward the smoldering ruin, and when he saw Virgil it was too late to stop his words. "Looking for someone?" the sheriff inquired quietly, and Trace could deny nothing.

"Have you seen him?" he gasped.

"All I've seen is what you're looking at. If the kid was in there, his troubles are over now."

Trace felt sick. He tried to get nearer to the cabin, or what was left of it, but Virgil's hand was like a vice on his shoulder. "Don't be a fool!" he snapped. "That porch roof is going any minute!"

"Maybe he got out," Trace said. "Douglas got out."

"What are you talking about? Who's Douglas?"

"Douglas Laurent! He came home just now with Danny's gun—the one he took off you, and he must have gotten it from the cabin. Danny had it with him when he went in there last night."

Trace looked about searchingly. There was only one other building in the canyon, and that one just a few running steps away. He had company on the run because now Virgil wasn't going to let him out of sight; but the barn was as empty as Danny had found it, and Trace had no time to study tire tracks. Out in the sunlight again he threw back his head and called out at the top of his voice, "Danny! Where are you, Dan-ny!" And a half a dozen echoes threw back the call.

A tongue of flame shot up higher at the taste of fresh timber, but only the crackling of the fire answered the echoes.

Nothing was left of the cabin now but the heavy porch floor and the burning uprights, and nothing would be left inside but the twisted ruin of the kerosene stove and a few black-objects of metal. Trace began to think of that now and to think too of what Douglas had said about the cabin. ". . . she won't use it any more. No one will ever use it now." At the edge of disaster a man got strange ideas, and when a little scrap of white something waved to him from the porch floor, he moved forward without thought of danger.

"You crazy idiot!" Virgil yelled. "Come away from there!"

But when Trace came away he had Francy's handkerchief in his hand.

A scrap of flimsy white cloth edged with cheap lace and embroidered with the letter F. F for Francy, F for failure. Now Trace understood just a little of what would have to be known to find the face of murder; but now it was too late. The cabin was gone and, as Douglas had said, everything in it. Was Danny gone too? He turned away from the cabin and began to search the canyon wall for some sign of move-ment on the rocks. Even if Danny had fallen asleep with a lighted cigarette he was young and fast enough to get out ahead of the fire—providing he was only asleep. It might take hours for that ruin behind him to cool enough for searching, but those same hours could mean another kind of death to a green kid lost in this canyon. . . .

Danny was no mountain climber. That hike across the desert after abandoning the sheriff's car couldn't be classed as a Sunday School outing, but at least the desert was level and as far down as a fellow could go. The earth didn't crumble under foot, and rocks didn't go bouncing down the dizzy descent just as you were about to put your weight on them. It wasn't such a deep canyon from the standpoint of the geography books, but it seemed to get deeper below and higher above the longer Danny climbed.

It was easier if he didn't look down. It was easier if he didn't look up and try to measure the distance to the top, if he just thought about one arm's length, one footing at a time. He should have gone back and tried to find the cabin and that narrow road the jeep had taken last night; but the man with Virgil Keep's gun was back there, and the skillet and the bloodstained towel. There was a limit to what Danny's nerves could stand. There must be a limit, too, to what his body could stand, but the body was a peculiar mechanism. Just when it seemed ready to give out and stop functioning, a new spurt of life would come like all the cylinders taking hold after a misfire. Danny kept climbing.

Sometimes he stopped to catch his breath and wipe the sweat off his face. The sun was burning a hole in the top of his head, and the only shade here was for snakes and lizards. Then he remembered what he'd been thinking up at that mining camp the day before: how nice it would be to escape civilization and get lost in these mountains. Well, this was it. This was the great freedom, pioneer fashion, but it was still the same old battle to keep alive. A different set of enemies were waiting for him—the rocks and the sun and the not so unlikely possibility that one of these boulders might break out into a nest of rattlesnakes, but the pay-off for losing was the same. It was right there below him, silent and peaceful like its name. Peace Canyon. Peace and death, the one thing man always sought, and the one thing he always found. Off in the distance something that appeared to be a cloud of smoke was rising up from the canyon floor, but Danny had no time to contemplate its origin. On he climbed, one arm's length, one footing at a time—the way man always had reached his desire. . . .

He didn't have to look up to know when he reached the rim; the rush of the wind told him. He crawled up over the edge and looked out over a world that had never looked so good. Columbus must have felt the same way when he sighted land . . . or those wagon-train immigrants of another century when they crawled out of the desert and saw pasturage ahead.

What stretched before Danny was not a boulevard, but he could walk now—run if he had the strength—and a ragged line of vegetation in the distance had to mean water in this country. He thought of that dry river the day before and his heart sank, but this was in the mountains and mountains had springs . . . at least that's what he promised himself all the way to that clump of foliage. He found a stream, a little stream that in one spot made a small pool where he could drink, bathe his face, and douse his head in the greatest orgy of his life. This stuff was better than vintage champagne; this stuff should be bottled and sold by the ounce! And on the bank of the stream was shade for resting in, and the wind blowing over his wet T.shirt was like an air cooler.

Danny didn't know it, but the stream he had found ran alongside the wagon-track trail leading to the now smoldering cabin. The first realization he had of the road was the sound of a motor approaching, and, exhausted and aching tired as he was, he scrambled for shelter behind the handiest bush. Moments later a light blue pickup rolled out of the dust and stopped a few yards away. Danny didn't dare raise his head, but he could hear someone getting out of the truck and threshing his way down to the spring; and then through the branches he caught a glimpse of a tall man in a wide hat. Jim Rice. This was the guy with the ready laughter and the warped sense of humor. He'd probably be convulsed at the sight of a dusty, sweat-stained fugitive in the bushes. The best bet was to remain hidden and keep silent, but that pickup was a tempting eyeful. Rice had left the door standing open on the driver's side, and Danny could see the sunlight flashing on the string of keys in the ignition.

The climb up the side of Peace Canyon must have made Danny reckless; not otherwise would he have dreamed of what he was planning now. Rice had finished getting his drink from the spring, but he didn't seem in any hurry to get back to his truck. Danny could see him more clearly now. He had walked a few steps farther away and was frowning up at that smoke cloud hanging over the canyon. Maybe he wasn't coming back for a while. He had a rifle slung under one arm; he might be going hunting. And then Danny remembered what new game was on open season these days, and his daring faded momentarily. . . . What if Rice was a part of the posse? . . . What if he happened to look down at the right spot and sight those fresh tracks in the soft earth around the spring? . . . A scrawny mountain bush wasn't going to be much protection against that rifle.

So it was six of one and half a dozen of another, and Danny chose the six. He waited for an instant when the tall man's back was turned and then ran from a crouching start.

He ran swift and low to the ground, making no more noise than the wind in the bushes or a pack rat in the night; but Jim Rice was an old hand at hunting and his ears were very sharp. Danny was almost even with the rear bumper when Rice whirled and raised his rifle.

It was the sunlight on the moving gun barrel that gave Danny warning. He dropped to the ground before Rice could get off his shot, and rolled in the dust to the far side of the truck. The right rear wheel made a good stopping place. Let Jim Rice put a bullet through his own tires if he wanted to do any shooting!

And then while the angry voice on the far side of the truck was yelling at him to step out with his hands up, Danny noticed something familiar about those tires. They had left the same tread marks on the dusty road as the ones he'd seen a couple of hours earlier on the floor of the barn in Peace Canyon.

Chapter Fifteen

"Well, if it ain't the wandering boy!" Rice drawled, as Danny raised up from behind the wheel. "Keep those hands up!"

"I haven't got a gun," Danny said.

"Oh, no! What did you do—leave it in Junction City?"

Jim Rice wasn't going to ease his grip on that rifle no matter what Danny told him, and Danny wasn't in a position to argue. They were standing just that way, eyeing each other like a pair of strange dogs, when another dust cloud rolled down the trail from Peace Canyon and settled down around the body of a red jeep. Never had company been so welcome. Undoubtedly that blue pickup didn't carry the only set of tires in the vicinity that would match the tread marks in that barn, but Danny was in no shape to rationalize at the moment. All he could think of were the bloodstains in the cabin, and all he'd heard about the death of a woman named Francy.

"Danny!" Trace called, hopping to the ground. "Are you all right?"

"Is *he* all right! Now isn't that thoughtful?" Rice said. "I catch an armed killer and you want to know if *he's* all right!"

"Danny isn't armed," Trace snapped.

"How do you know?"

"Never mind how I know. What happened, Danny? What happened back in that cabin?"

It was a question Danny would have liked to answer, complete with descriptive passages, but two things happened to stop him. One was the sudden arrival of Virgil Keep, who wasn't letting Trace Cooper out of his sight any more, and the other was the delayed reaction of a two-day flight to nowhere that had finally brought him back to the long and strong arm of the law. Danny's arms weren't strong at all any more, and his legs were like strings of wet spaghetti. He grabbed the door handle of the truck for support, and saw Rice's rifle swing toward his head.

"Put that damn gun down!" Trace shouted. "Can't you see the kid's done in?"

"What do you want me to do," Rice demanded, "hold his hand?"

"Just hold your fire! You don't have to worry about Danny now, Jim. The sheriff's here; he'll take charge."

Danny couldn't account for it, but somehow even that big ugly sheriff didn't look too bad. Maybe he was just too far gone to be afraid, or maybe he was just too afraid to know it; but he crawled into Virgil's borrowed car about the way he would have crawled into a feather bed if there'd been one handy. They were going back to Cooperton now, Danny and the sheriff and Trace following along behind in the jeep; but Jim Rice couldn't wait for the procession. With a pointed suggestion that perhaps the sheriff should wait until he sent back a few deputies to protect him from so dangerous a prisoner, he tore off down the trail ahead like Paul Revere with a red-hot tip about the British. Jim wanted to be sure the party had a reception committee, and that nobody got the story of this capture secondhand.

Practically all of Cooperton came down to the sheriff's office to welcome back Danny Ross, and they weren't there to give him the keys to the city. Danny was still too exhausted to be more than vaguely aware of what was going on, but he gathered that he wasn't going to win any popularity contest with this crowd. Virgil had picked up a deputy and a photographer at the intersection where the canyon road met the highway, and together with Trace they formed a pretty formidable bodyguard. The photographer was a man from the D.A.'s office, and the intersection, Danny learned on the way in, was the spot where Francy Allen had been found. This piece of information fitted in nicely with what he'd seen in that cabin, and somebody should know about it; but the sidewalk was rolling like a choppy sea, and the steps up to Virgil's office had about six-foot risers.

"Somebody telephone Dr. Glenn," he heard the sheriff say off in the distance, and then everybody went away for a while and left Danny in the darkness. . . .

About the time Danny collapsed, a big black man in a light suit elbowed his way through the crowd outside the sheriff's office and began asking for Trace Cooper. He might as well have saved his breath, because nobody was listening to anything but the sound of his own anger anyway; but when Trace suddenly appeared in the doorway, Arthur waved down his attention.

"Trace," he called. "Hey, Trace, I'm back."

Arthur was like a bonus from fate. Lowell Glenn's office phone rang without response, and Virgil wouldn't hear of calling old Doc Gaynor's residence on a day such as this. It was nice and respectable of Virgil, but in Trace's book the living took precedence over the dead any day. In very few words he explained what he wanted Arthur to do.

"But don't you want to hear what I found out in Red Rock?" Arthur protested.

"Just as soon as you get Glenn over here," Trace said. "I don't think the kid's suffering from anything more than sunburn and exhaustion, but it might calm down a few excited citizens if they see he needs a doctor. It's not much fun to lynch someone too sick to care."

Trace might have exaggerated the temper of the crowd—it was too early to tell—but it did seem that every man, woman, and child in Cooperton, with two exceptions, were either in front of the sheriff's office or on the way over. And that old truck coming down the street was Walter Wade's, with Viola leaning her head out of the cab so as not to miss any of the excitement.

"O.K.," Arthur said, "but in case you can't wait the answer is yes."

Now, of course, Danny Ross didn't hear any of this conversation, and it wouldn't have made sense to him anyway. It wouldn't have made sense to the crowd either, who were just being normally curious about a desperate killer with two murder charges hanging over him. Two—and if you listened to Viola Wade (it was quite a feat to avoid listening), maybe three. Cooperton was of a mind to believe anything at this point, considering those two fresh graves in the cemetery and that new addition to the Junction City morgue.

But there were two people in Cooperton who didn't know a thing about all this excitement until Arthur stuck his thumb on the Gaynor doorbell. Through the fancy glass panels on the old-fashioned door, he saw Joyce rise from the sofa and come forward. Trace was right: she wasn't alone, and the other occupant of the sofa was young Doctor Glenn. At the hearing of Arthur's message, he bounded up like a trial lawyer making an objection.

"The sheriff's office!" he echoed. "Why am I wanted there?"

"Sick boy," Arthur said. "They just brought in Danny Ross. He's kind of done in."

It seemed to be a letdown for the doctor, or maybe a relief; but he wasn't taking Arthur's word for anything. "This sounds like some of Trace Cooper's doings," he said. "Why didn't Virgil telephone if he wanted me?"

"He did. You weren't in."

"There's a phone in this house, too!"

"Sure there is," Arthur agreed, "so why don't you just ring up the sheriff and see if I'm telling the truth."

Arthur waited in the hall where the afternoon sun cast long shadows on the faded carpet, and where Lowell Glenn's struggle for an open line came like an impatient staccato from the old doctor's study. The telephone operator would be pretty busy for a while helping the countryside catch up on the latest news. Joyce stood by the door, pale and troubled.

"Was he hurt when they took him?" she asked.

"Who—Danny Ross?"

"Yes. Trace thinks he's innocent."

"Was Trace here?"

"A few hours ago."

That accounted for the doctor's reluctance to leave, Arthur decided. He probably suspected the whole thing was a trick to get him out of the house so Trace could return. "The doctor sure hates to see you two get together," he remarked, nodding toward the study door. "He must be afraid Trace is going to talk some sense into your head." He expected Joyce to rare up and protest this intrusion in what she considered a private affair, but all the fight was gone out of Joyce now. She was still wearing black, and her pale blond hair was all done up in a sedate style that suited her about like jodhpurs on a cowpoke. It was the dress of mourning, but there was more worry than grief in her eyes.

"What is 'sense'?" she asked hollowly. "I've given up trying to rationalize anything. I just don't understand, Arthur. I don't understand murder, and I don't understand deceit. Why do people do such terrible things?"

"Maybe they don't mean the things they do to be terrible," Arthur said. "Maybe they mean them for good and they turn out wrong."

"You're talking about Trace and Francy, aren't you?"

"I'm just talking about the things people do. Take your grandfather, for instance. I don't suppose there ever was a finer man, but that didn't stop him from making a terrible mistake."

Joyce's head came up quickly. She was trying to read answers in Arthur's face, but he was heir to an old silence that volunteered nothing. And he was loyal. That's why he holds me in such contempt, she thought—he's loyal and I'm not.

"You've got to tell me," she said. "You were on the place all the time Francy was there; you must know the truth."

"I'd be the smartest man on earth if I did," Arthur muttered.

"Don't talk like that! It's all very noble of you to keep silent because Trace does and you respect his wishes, but it's not for myself that I'm asking. Can't you see what's happening? People are beginning to say that Francy was murdered just like my grandfather. If it turns out that Danny Ross isn't guilty, who do you suppose will be accused next?"

All the fear in Joyce's eyes had a name now, but Arthur couldn't protest. He couldn't answer or make any denial, because now Lowell Glenn had completed his call and was putting down the phone. There was only a moment before he came back into the hall, hat in hand, and in that moment it was Joyce who spoke.

"I wouldn't blame him if he did kill her," she said. "If all we've suffered is a lie and she let it go on, I wish I had killed her myself."

The answer was yes—that's what Arthur had called back as he edged back through the crowd. Trace took the knowledge back inside with him, but by this time it was more of a corroboration than a surprise. The inkstains on Francy's fingers had to mean what he now knew: she had regained consciousness before her death; she had been able to use a pen. But Francy had no worldly goods to bestow, and she couldn't have been writing her memoirs so close to the edge of her grave. What she could have done was sign a statement and name a name only one other person could have known until it was shared with Charley Gaynor.

So it all came back to the old man as Trace knew it must. But where was the statement now? Had the doctor made an extra stop on the road back to Cooperton? Had he posted a letter or made a telephone call? The latter idea Trace abandoned immediately. Any act the doctor might have performed was still a deep secret, and conversations on the Cooperton line were as confidential as a bass drum. Trace pondered that unhappy fact for a moment, and then he began to understand.

But conjecture was foolish until Arthur returned with the details, and even when he returned, with a grumbling Lowell Glenn in tow, the outlook didn't brighten. No one at the hospital had any knowledge of a written statement. All Arthur had learned was that Francy had been conscious before her death, and that the old doctor was closeted with her until the last. It was like finding a key only to realize that the door was still missing.

113

"What are you two hanging around for?" Virgil demanded, returning from Danny's cell. "Lowell says there's nothing wrong with the kid but some blisters and scratches."

"Can I talk to him?" Trace asked.

"Why should you?"

What Trace really wanted was to pry out of Danny every word Charley Gaynor had uttered during their brief acquaintance. Words that meant nothing to him might mean a great deal to a man with a key. But he wasn't ready to share this new found knowledge just yet.

"I'd like to know how that fire started in the cabin," he said.

"I'll write you a letter when I find out."

"Virgil, for God's sake be reasonable!"

"I am being reasonable! I'm letting you walk out of here instead of throwing you into a cell where you belong. I know how the kid got to that cabin, and you know damn well that I do! If it was anyone else—"

Virgil didn't get any farther. A cry from the street interrupted his tirade. . . . "Hey, Virgil, what's the doc for? You going to pretty up the kid for his funeral?"

"Break it up out there!" Virgil yelled. "Everybody go on home!"

The deputy at the door squinted through the glass panel. "Nobody's going," he said. "That's Jim Rice shooting off his mouth. I think he's been drinking."

"Well, tell him to go home!"

"I've got a better idea," Trace said. "Ask him to come in."

Both Virgil and the deputy looked at Trace as if he'd gone mad, but there was nothing wrong with his reasoning. Jim Rice on the inside couldn't cause any trouble on the outside. "Get the Wades in here, too," he ordered. "There's something I want to ask them."

Nothing Virgil had said seemed to discourage Trace. Straddle-legged and confident, with his red hair tossed high as a gamecock's comb, this run-down relic of the past possessed more authority in the lift of his eyebrow than Virgil Keep could command with a scepter. Virgil wasn't afraid of the crowd, drunk or sober. Crowds were like cattle, docile enough if you knew how to ride herd; but Trace was a maverick who wore no man's brand, and he wasn't leaving.

"What do you want to ask?" he queried.

"About murder. You can listen if you wish."

Trace turned his back on the office and took the few steps to the cell where Lowell Glenn was swabbing disinfectant on Danny's bruised hands. The kid had been out only a few minutes, but he still had an eerie pallor under his sunburn. He frowned back at Trace's frown, and then peered over his shoulder at the several people coming into the sheriff's office. Jim Rice, Viola and Walter Wade—together with Danny they comprised the sole survivors of that last call Charley Gaynor made at Mountain View, and that's just what Trace wanted. If they rehashed every detail, every word and action, he might pick up some clue; if not, he might at least plant a few doubts in the place of this cocksure acceptance of Danny's guilt. Walter would be easy to shake; give him an argument and Walter Wade wasn't certain of his own name; but the other two would be tough customers. Jim Rice because he hated all Coopers, past and present, and Viola because she lived with a big imagination in a little world.

But to Danny, sitting bolt upright on the edge of the cell cot, they were all like spectators at the zoo. What was Danny Ross in their eyes—a monkey, a tiger, or just a goat? Maybe he should make that a mountain goat after this afternoon's climb; and then Danny remembered what it was he'd been climbing from, and what he had to tell Trace.

"The cabin," he began. "Tell the sheriff to look in the cabin!"

There was no need to relay the message. "The cabin's burned down," Virgil said.

"Burned down!"

Danny sank back against the wall. He should have kept his mouth shut. He should have waited for somebody else to start the talking; but once he'd stuck his neck out so far there was no stopping the questions.

"Why should Virgil look in the cabin?" Trace demanded. "What happened back there, Danny? How did that fire get started?"

"I don't know! I didn't know there was a fire!"

"He was running from it fast enough when I caught him," Jim drawled.

Nobody invited Jim to horn in. He came shoving forward like a man on a free pass, and the drinks he'd hoisted while relating his exploit to the boys at the Pioneer bar gave his blue eyes a cruel and glassy stare. He laughed, and that was the finish.

Danny wasn't tired any more. He was on his feet like a bristling cat, and no matter if the pasty-faced doctor did get an elbow in his bifocals. For two days Danny had been hounded, and for two days he'd trembled, hidden, and run for his life; but the time had come when he couldn't run any more—wouldn't run even if somebody turned the key and swung open those barred doors! All the way up that canyon wall he'd faced a dozen deaths more terrible than anything these leering faces could threaten—and they were all leering faces: Jim Rice, the sheriff, that big-bosomed woman with the greasy hair. Even Trace was a stranger now, because what could he make of a guy who would take him to a place like that cabin and leave him like a fish in a barrel? Danny hated them all.

"You shut your trap!" he yelled. "All of you—you hear me? I'm fed up with being blamed for things I never did! I wasn't running from any fire because I didn't even know there was a fire, but I do know what was in that cabin— blood! Dried blood on the floor, on the skillet, and all over that towel! And clothes—ladies' clothes, and tire marks on the barn floor just like the treads on this guy's truck!"

Danny's words spilled out like colts breaking through a corral, and when his voice stopped he felt lonesome and surprised. He'd shouted at them louder than they shouted at him. He wasn't afraid any more.

Jim backed up a step as if he'd caught a blow on the chin. "You lying bastard!" he howled. "Listen to him lie! Listen to him covering up!"

"Take it easy," Trace said. "Maybe he isn't lying."

"The hell he ain't! You heard him trying to throw blame on me, and you're just as bad! How come you always side with the kid, I want to know? How come you're so dead sure he's innocent?"

"Shut up, both of you!" Virgil snapped. "I want to hear

116

what the kid has to say. What's all this about bloodstains?"

And so Danny finally got the chance to have his say. It was easy: all you had to do was yell loud enough and people backed up and listened. Everybody listened, even Jim Rice. Slowly and carefully he told them all about the bloodstains in the cabin, the big one on the floor, and the trail out to the porch, and then he took them all out to the barn with him to hear about those tire marks in the dust. Nobody interrupted Danny now. They were too interested in hearing about that man waiting in the cabin when he returned. The man with the short temper and Virgil's gun.

"He started yelling about people using his cabin all the time," Danny said. "He told me to clear out and take all that junk in the dresser—clothes, ladies' underclothes mostly, and that's when we found the iron skillet with a bloody towel wrapped around it and yellow hairs matted on the edge."

It was a dandy story the way Danny told it, and he had a fascinated audience all the way from the doctor inside the cell to the deputy who was supposed to be watching that street door. But the deputy wasn't watching, and he didn't see the man who came in while Danny talked. Even Danny didn't see him come in. He just stopped for breath and looked up, and there the man was listening as intently as the rest.

Danny couldn't think of another word. He'd never seen the newcomer before, and yet there was something awfully familiar about his appearance. Maybe it was the gun he was drawing from his coat pocket.

Chapter Sixteen

"Good evening, sheriff," said Alexander Laurent. "I believe this revolver belongs to you."

His voice was like the pipe organ coming on after a noisy soap opera. Every eye turned to meet him.

"I must apologize for not speaking up sooner," he added, "but I was intrigued by the young man's story. Danny Ross, isn't it?"

Nobody answered. They were all too busy staring at this remarkable man: remarkable because he didn't belong in a world of dusty hats and faded levis, and because he didn't seem to mind a bit. His deep-set eyes swept the office, taking in everyone from the deputy at his shoulder to the timid Ada edging forward along the cell-block hall, and Danny had the feeling they were all being X-rayed and catalogued in one brief glance. He just about had this stranger tabbed when Virgil spoke up and clinched the identification.

"It's my gun all right, Mr. Laurent," he said, "but how the devil did you get it?"

"From my son—the man Danny Ross encountered in the cabin."

So this was Laurent! Danny took a good look this time, remembering what Trace had told him. Laurent was on his side, and it was his son he'd faced in the cabin. That made the familiarity easy to understand: the same fine features, the same hairline, the same height. But there was nothing boyish about the elder Laurent, and he didn't need a gun in his hand to make him impressive. With a careless gesture he handed the weapon to Virgil.

"You'll notice that one shot has been fired," he added. "That's how your mysterious fire began. When young Mr. Ross threw an armful of clothing in Douglas's face, the gun discharged and ignited a kerosene lamp on the table. But I suppose you're wondering what Douglas was doing in the cabin in the first place."

Laurent smiled briefly, and there wasn't a soul in the place who could give him an argument on that statement. Danny was forgotten now; nobody cared to visit the zoo. When Dr. Glenn picked up his satchel and left the cell (locking it behind him), Danny was left the only outsider to this strange convention. He felt like an eavesdropper.

"For some time," Laurent continued, "there has been evidence of trespassing at the cabin. Empty food tins and bottles have been found on the premises, and the ranch hands have reported seeing a light in the canyon at night. These things were never reported to you, sheriff, because we weren't using the cabin anyway and I saw no harm in an occasional uninvited guest. Yesterday, however, my son went out to look the place over to see if it would be suitable for a personal retreat as Mr. Cooper had suggested. He made the natural error of taking Danny to be our visitor."

Everybody else may have been satisfied with this explanation, but Danny wasn't. "I don't wear ladies clothes!" he shouted from the cell. "I don't use face cream and perfume!"

"I doubt if Douglas identified those articles. His temper is a bit explosive, I'm afraid."

"He identified them all right! He kept talking about some woman he didn't want hanging around any more!"

For the first time Alexander Laurent lost a little of his poise. This was Danny's day to hurl charges, and he was making the most of it. With that muttering crowd outside there might not be another one.

"It was a woman using the cabin," he repeated, "and I know who it was. I've heard you all talking about somebody named Francy Allen. Well, I saw a handkerchief out there and it had an F in the corner."

"Like this?" Trace asked.

When Danny saw the object Trace took out of his pocket, he could stop shouting. It was the handkerchief, and now they could all see it. They could hear him explain how he'd picked it up on that burning porch, and they could reach their own conclusions. It wasn't difficult to understand that crowd outside. Murderer wasn't a nice word to fasten on a neighbor; it was much easier to follow Viola's line and put the blame on a stranger. But if Francy Allen had been hit with an iron skillet instead of an automobile and then left on the highway to die, it meant that murder had come to Cooperton a good twelve hours ahead of Danny Ross.

"What about that?" Virgil demanded of Laurent. "Did your son know who was using the cabin?"

"He couldn't have known," Laurent retorted indignantly. "My son isn't well. That's why I brought him to this climate in the first place. He doesn't carry on social activities."

It was about time for Jim Rice to laugh, and he delivered on schedule. "Social activities!" he howled. "That's a new name for it! You can't be too sure about the young fellows, Mr. Laurent. Maybe Virgil should have a talk with Douglas."

"By all means," Laurent agreed amiably, "and on the way

to the ranch he can stop and have a look at those tire marks in the barn. My son doesn't drive, you see, but it must be obvious even to you that Miss Allen required transportation to any rendezvous she might have kept in the cabin—especially on the return trip."

It wasn't Laurent's words so much as his pointed manner that set Jim off, but the combination was like putting a torch to a haystack. Jim's face turned as red as the sunset outside the west windows. "Tire tracks don't mean anything!" he protested. "I buy my tires from Walter. I'll bet he sells plenty of those tires. I'll bet he uses them himself."

"Tires?" Walter echoed freely. "What tires? What's everybody talking about?"

"About Francy," Viola screamed in his ear. "She was murdered after all, just like I said. I told you a woman like Francy wouldn't die by accident!"

Viola was only putting into words what they were all thinking by this time, but the words sounded cold and naked and brought a moment of terrible silence. From where Danny stood, gripping the bars with both hands, everyone in the office looked a bit frightened at the realization. It was beautiful to see these self-assured people beginning to doubt. It was wonderful to hear them scratching for cover. And in the hall just outside the cell door, the reticent Ada gasped and turned pale.

"Is that true?" she cried out. "Is that really what happened to Francy?"

With the exception of Danny no one had previously been aware of the woman's presence. It was the moment of surprise that gave her the opportunity to continue.

"If it's true then I have to tell," she said. "Murder is a terrible sin."

No one ever paid heed to Ada. If she spoke her words were lost in the current of conversation; if she remained silent her silence was that of a door, or a wall, or any unseeing, unthinking object. But now Ada had an audience, and before it her voice became strained and self-conscious as if she struggled with an unfamiliar tongue.

"I have to tell about Jim and Francy," she said. "They were carrying on—"

"That's a damned lie!" Jim exploded, but now that Ada had found her tongue she wouldn't be shouted down. "I knew for a long time," she continued, "but I didn't say anything on account of Ethel being so poorly. I didn't want her to fret."

Of that stunned audience only Trace seemed able to respond. "How long a time?" he demanded.

Ada frowned over her answer. "I can't rightly say, Mr. Cooper—as long as I've been walking out nights. Oh, they're the smart ones all right, meeting down by the cemetery so's nobody would know, but somebody always knows. No matter what we do, somebody knows." The trouble deep in Ada's eyes seemed old and unconcerned with Jim and Francy Allen, but then she returned from the land of her fancy to complete her quiet indictment. "The important thing," she said, "is that I saw them together the night before Francy died. It was real late so they weren't even being careful, and I saw Jim put Francy into the cab of his truck. She was acting peculiar. I thought she was drunk."

"She was drunk!" Jim yelled, and a little victory smile touched Ada's lips. You see, it seemed to say, I did have something to say after all.

But now the audience was all Jim's. A few moments earlier he'd been a bit drunk himself, but now he sobered under the impact of his own words. A mousy little woman and his own big mouth—that combination was too much to fight. He backed up against the wall and seemed to be groping for an escape behind the plaster.

"All right," he said thickly, "I admit seeing Francy that night. We had a few drinks together. I'd just made a deal with that cattle buyer and was feeling good. A man has to feel good once in a while even if his wife is ailing!"

Nobody was arguing with Jim. Nobody said anything at all.

"Francy never could hold her liquor," he added. "I couldn't take her back to her rooming house drunk; she'd have been chucked out; so I put her in my truck and drove her out to the cabin."

"Was that the usual procedure?" Trace asked.

"It's none of your damn business if it was! I never heard of you being any plaster saint!"

121

Jim wiped his sweaty face with one hand and tried to remember what else he had to say. All those faces, all those eyes were still waiting. There must be something more. "She was all right when I left her," he said. "She was sleeping it off quiet as you please. When I heard about her being found on the road next morning, I figured she'd woke up and tried to walk back to town. She could have walked into the side of a truck the shape she was in and never known it."

Jim paused and thought things over. "For all I know yet, that's just what happened," he added.

"You're forgetting the bloodstains," Virgil said.

"I'm forgetting nothing! I never saw any bloodstains, and now there ain't any place to see them! And all I've heard about bloodstains is from Danny Ross and his extra-smart lawyer. How do you know this ain't some trick they've cooked up to get everybody excited over Francy and forget all about poor old Doc Gaynor?"

Jim's meaning was clear. Laurent's an outsider, he was saying; Laurent's a tricky lawyer with a big reputation for getting accused killers off scot free. He looked to Walter and Viola for support, but Walter's jaw seemed permanently unhinged, and Viola was too thrilled over the prospect of a new item for the party line even to remember which side she was on. Jim didn't seem to have a friend in the place, but he did have an enemy . . . a redheaded enemy with a pair of fists clenched big as cabbages.

"So it was you!" Trace exclaimed. "I ought to break your damned neck!"

One of those fists was already on its way to Jim's jaw, but the strong arms of Arthur stopped Trace on the brink of mayhem. "Gentlemen!" Laurent cried. "You can't settle anything with violence. You must have facts!"

"I'll give you facts!" Trace shouted. "I'll give all of you a few facts you never heard before! Fact number one: Francy didn't die in a coma as we all thought. She was conscious and closeted with Doctor Gaynor for ten or fifteen minutes before her death. Fact number two: during that time she used Charley's leaky pen to sign something and got ink on the fingers of her right hand. You can check on the first fact at the hospital, just as Arthur did today, and the other can be verified by calling Fisher's mortuary."

Trace had blurted out the whole story at once. He paused and looked about him. "Whatever it was that Francy signed is now conspicuously missing," he added, "but she wasn't the type to forgive her own murderer!"

Danny was learning something new every minute—not only about a dying woman and her inkstained fingers, but about the telltale marks on the living. Within a matter of moments a loudmouth who laughed at the wrong places had lost his sense of humor, and Trace Cooper, who hadn't seemed to have a nerve in his body, had to be restrained by a pair of strong black arms and the tongue of an old man. Alexander Laurent looked even older now, but so did everybody else.

"I hesitate to criticize," he interrupted, "but isn't fact number two tainted with conjecture?"

"There's nothing wrong with conjecture if it's logical," Trace snapped. "Figure it out for yourself. Francy was in somebody's way. She wasn't wanted any more, and dead women don't write memoirs, but Francy was a rugged kid who took a lot of killing. She was left for dead on the highway to make her death appear an accident, but she didn't die soon enough. We were all anxious to know how she came out when Charley took her to Red Rock, but one person must have been a lot more than anxious."

With words for weapons Trace didn't need fists. He shrugged off Arthur's grip and continued.

"Now we come to the interesting part of the story. Francy's dead, and everybody knows it because old Charley called Fisher on the party line; but nobody knows whether or not she talked before she died. Nobody but Charley, and he's driving home to Cooperton. But first Charley has to make that stop at Mountain View that was his regular routine when he'd been away from his office most of the day. Anyone who knew Charley knew that."

Trace's voice was no less commanding than that of his silver-haired mentor, and back in that tiny cell Danny was hanging on every word. The words were becoming a memory, a memory of an old man with a strange way of talking as if the worry on his mind blotted out all the usual small talk between strangers. Danny tried to recall just exactly what it was the old doctor had said during that brief acquaintance, but Trace was talking again, and he had to listen.

"Under those circumstances, I imagine it would be a little difficult for Francy's murderer to stay away from Mountain View," he said.

"That narrows the field of suspects," Laurent observed. "There were only four people waiting at Mountain View when the doctor arrived."

"Only four?" Trace paused, his shaggy red eyebrows pushing up on the bridge of his nose. "What about the car Danny says he heard pulling away as the bus left?"

"Danny says!" Jim interrupted. "Who cares what Danny says? You'd think he was judge and jury instead of a young thug who slugged the sheriff and pushed a gun in the ribs of some poor devil down in Junction City!"

The trouble with Jim was that his feelings were hurt. Here he'd gone and captured the escaped killer the whole state was looking for, and instead of thanks he received only accusations and innuendoes. "I wouldn't belittle Danny's hypothetical car if I were you," Trace cautioned. "If there wasn't any car, then, as Mr. Laurent suggests, we have narrowed the field of suspects. . . . But suppose there was a car, and suppose our person unknown was having a heart-to-heart talk with Charley Gaynor when Steve Malone came around the corner of the café."

Trace was painting a picture again, and without live models it was vague and shadowy. Danny tried to see it, but it didn't come clear. There was something else he had to remember about Steve Malone before the picture moved to Junction City.

Nobody else had trouble seeing the picture, particularly Alexander Laurent. "The only weakness in your theory, Mr. Cooper," he remarked, "is that we find ourselves with approximately nine hundred and ninety-seven possible murderers."

"Francy didn't have that many friends," Trace objected.

"I wasn't confining the count to friends. For every admirer we must multiply by two—the jealous wife, the troubled fiancée; or possibly by three—the eternal triangle. Oh, you've given us a splendid motive for the old doctor's murder, and a fine reason for the sudden demise of Mr. Malone;

but aren't we in need of a motive for Miss Allen's death? Assuming, of course, that she actually was murdered."

"I gave you a motive!"

"A motive," Laurent repeated, "but only one of many possibilities. Now what would you say to the motive of a young man whose life had been shattered by a lie?"

"That wasn't Francy's fault!" Trace cried.

"Wasn't it? Why don't you ask Dr. Glenn about that? Isn't it true, doctor, that Miss Allen came first to you and only went to Red Rock when you refused the services she sought? And isn't it also true that you went straightway to Dr. Gaynor and reported that she had named Trace Cooper as the father of her unborn child?"

"Francy wouldn't have said that!"

Laurent shook his head sadly. "Mr. Cooper," he scolded, "I'm disappointed in you. When are you going to stop creating people in your own image and likeness? Because you thought of Miss Allen as a sisterly charge, does it necessarily follow that she thought of you as a big brother?" Laurent's eyes sought Arthur in that ring of faces, Arthur whose dark countenance never gave away secrets. But there was a glint of recognition when their eyes met, and Laurent smiled. "There's more than one way to remove a rival from the field," he murmured. "But then, I never attempt to explain the things women do: why Mrs. Keep doesn't sleep well, for instance, or why Mrs. Wade evidences such delight in murder. Insofar as possible, I try to avoid conjecture and adhere strictly to the facts."

Laurent made a little tent of his long fingers and contemplated the structure thoughtfully.

"The facts," he added, "are rather discouraging. Any of us, any of us in this very room, could have murdered both Miss Allen and the doctor. We could have acted from motives unknown, from circumstances beyond our control. The thing to remember is that the first two deaths were by means of the handiest instrument possible, as if unpremeditated, whereas Mr. Malone was very neatly dispatched with a bullet in the forehead. This not only bears out Mr. Cooper's theory that Malone was a marked man, but it gives us our first positive link to the murderer. . . . Who has the gun that killed Steve Malone?"

Everyone looked at the weapon in Virgil's hand, even Danny. A gun in the hand was worth a dozen theories in the bush.

"It couldn't have been that gun," Trace insisted. "That gun wasn't fired."

Virgil checked the chamber. "It's been fired," he said.

"By Douglas in the cabin. It wasn't fired last night in that hotel room."

It took all of thirty seconds for Virgil to realize what Trace had said; Danny caught on in half the time. "Who told you Malone was shot in a hotel room?" the sheriff demanded, and then it had to come out. It had to all come out where it hurt the most. Danny followed Trace's reluctant rehearsal of their strange meeting at Malone's death bed with a sinking heart. Once Virgil had him fixed in that murder room nothing was going to get him out of this mess. He could see it written all over Virgil's face even before his outburst.

"Damn you, Trace, I'll have you in court for this and I don't care if the county is named after your grandad!" Virgil swore. "I warned you not to push me too far! Facts, the man says, facts!"

Alexander Laurent held no glory for Virgil. He was just a stranger with fancy clothes, fancy manners, and too many words. Now he could add a few of Virgil's to his collection.

"I've got a lump on my head, that's a fact! I've got a wrecked car that's been found in the bottom of a dry river just off the old road to Junction City, and I've got a report that Malone was shot with a forty-five. This is no water pistol that I'm holding. If that's not facts enough, I'll give you another one. I've got Danny Ross locked in a cell, and he's going to stay there until a court of law sets him free! Now clear out of here, all of you! This is no town hall!"

A less-talented man would have had to practice a long time for such a demonstration of wrath. Walter scurried for the door like a schoolboy at the closing bell, and Jim didn't seem to need a second invitation. But Trace resisted.

"What about those bloodstains in the cabin?" he demanded. "Aren't you going to do anything about them?"

Virgil's smile was as warm as a spinster's kiss. "Sure I am," he responded. "Just bring them in and I'll get out my magnifying glass and chemistry set. Bring along those inkstains, too, and that statement Francy is supposed to have written that tells us the name of her murderer. I'm surprised that a couple of smart men like you and Mr. Laurent haven't come up with that long ago. All you need is a sample of Francy's handwriting and a piece of paper!"

Virgil didn't intend his words to be inspiring; they weren't meant to be anything but the walking papers for two annoying visitors. But in the little digestive silence that followed Danny sucked in his breath audibly. A piece of paper! No other choice of words could have had such an effect. It was like a lever thrown or a button pressed, and the picture Trace's theory had begun to form came clear at last. A piece of paper!

But now everybody was leaving, and Danny couldn't have that. "Wait a minute!" he yelled. "Wait! I've got something to say!"

Chapter Seventeen

Danny hardly recognized the sound of his own voice. It was strangely authoritative—as if he really knew what he was going to say—and the response was a complete halt to that exodus toward the door. Now the anxious eyes were his to ponder.

"Well," Virgil growled, "what is it? What's on your mind?"

"Maybe he wants to confess," Jim said.

Danny looked at both men, each in turn. Jim really wasn't so tall after all, it was the hat that made him look that way; and Virgil's eyes were almost level with Danny's own. The discovery seemed significant at the time, but that wasn't what he'd called them back to discuss.

"There was a piece of paper," he said. "Doctor Gaynor had it in his wallet—a long folded sheet like a letter without an envelope."

Virgil looked troubled. "Did you see the wallet?" he snapped.

"Sure I saw it. We all saw it—Mr. Rice, Walter Wade, that big-mouthed wife of his—"

"Big-mouthed! I like that!" Viola shrieked.

"I guess you do, else you'd shut up," Danny said. "But it seems that people who hear so much should see a little too. How come nobody but me remembers that paper? It was in plain sight when it fell out of the old man's wallet while he was putting away that two hundred."

"When it fell out—" Laurent repeated. "Did the doctor retrieve it?"

"Malone did. I reached for it, but Malone was too quick for me. He looked kind of disappointed that it wasn't money."

"But he did return it to the doctor?"

"Sure he did. Like I said, it wasn't money."

Laurent could ask the questions, but Danny was watching Virgil. Virgil was the man with the key to the cell, and he wasn't going to buy this story either unless somebody started remembering along with Danny. It was Walter who obliged.

"Seems to me I recollect that paper," he mused. "Of course, there's no telling what was on it."

"Or where it went to," Viola added quickly.

"It went into the wallet," Danny said, "and the wallet went into the old man's coat pocket. Everybody could see that, too."

Everybody could see a lot of things now. They could see the excitement on Danny's face (all that color wasn't sunburn), and they could see the way he gripped the bars of the cell door until his knuckles turned white. The picture of that afternoon at Mountain View was complete now: every shape, every shadow, every movement. Even the acts he hadn't witnessed were beginning to take form like mountains poking through the raveled scarf of morning fog. The paper went into the wallet, the wallet went into the coat pocket, and the coat pocket was hung on the spotlight of an old sedan that needed a little attention under the hood.

For two days Danny had thought of a little man in a raincoat as being a murderer, so that finding him dead was like losing contact with reality and being plunged into headlong flight. But now he could see what none of the others had yet realized: that a man like Steve Malone would reach for money if the reach wasn't too far, but he'd never kill for it

128

or take dangerous risks. A pickpocket doesn't make a souvenir of the evidence of his theft, and what Francy Allen's murderer was looking for wouldn't have interested Malone any more than that wallet once the cash was removed.

"What is it son? What have you remembered?"

Laurent's voice was coaxing Danny back to the present. What had he remembered? Nothing really. Some things didn't have to be remembered, only recognized. Maybe the reason it was so easy to know what Steve Malone would have done was because Danny Ross might have done the same thing a few days ago. He could even recognize that now and recall his own feelings at the sight of all that money in the old doctor's hands.

"You better prompt him again," Jim muttered. "The kid doesn't seem to remember his lines."

Despite Jim's sarcasm, everybody was waiting for Danny's next words. He could read the anxiety in their eyes, and it flashed like a danger signal through his brain. What was it Laurent had said? "Any one of us in this very room could have murdered . . ." Any one. Any one of them could have gone searching for Steve Malone, because any one of them could have known Danny wasn't lying about the wallet. And now they were all waiting for him to tell them where it could be found!

"Let me out of here!" Danny cried. "Let me out for an hour and I'll give you your murderer!"

It was a wild declaration to make, but this was no time for conservatism. "Are you crazy?" Virgil gasped, but Danny had an answer for that. "Not crazy enough to tell everything I know!" he retorted. "I stand here listening to you guys making cracks at each other, and for a while I think the only difference between us is that you're out and I'm in; but then I get to wondering. Suppose I had killed the old man and somebody else was sitting in this cell in my place, wouldn't I get curious to see how he was taking it? Wouldn't I get nervous that maybe he'd wriggle off the hook and maybe I'd get stuck with it after all?"

"The worm is turning," Laurent observed. "The accused accuses."

"Why shouldn't I accuse? Nobody was bashful about

pinning this mess on me just because I had a couple of hundred bucks!"

"And plenty of opportunity," Virgil remarked.

"Sure, plenty of opportunity—just like the Wades and this guy Rice. Just like Mr. Cooper down in Junction City last night."

"My God," Trace gasped, "he even suspects me!"

"I suspect everybody!"

"Which is all very well up to a certain point," Laurent said, "but if you know something that will clear up this case you'll have to trust somebody. I'm offering my services as your lawyer, Danny."

"Why?" Danny demanded. "You don't owe me anything!"

"Every man owes something to every other man."

"Then go bankrupt! I'm not telling anybody anything, but if the sheriff unlocks this door I'll get that piece of paper! I'll get it and every one of you can come along and watch!"

Danny was shouting the last words, as if shouting would give weight to a hopeless argument. Virgil wouldn't go for it, the crowd outside wouldn't go for it, but now everything was as clear to Danny as if he'd lifted that wallet himself.

"The hell you will!" Virgil snapped. "If you've got anything to say, you can say it to me!"

"I've said all I have to say," Danny retorted.

"Then you can sit in that cell until you rot!"

This time Virgil was all through with argument. There was a door between the office and the cell block, a heavy slab door that slammed shut like an exclamation point after his words. The walls shook a little, and the conversation beyond the door fell away to murmurs. This wasn't what Danny had counted on. Somebody should have kept the ball rolling. Somebody should have asked a lot of questions about what he'd remembered just so he could get a line on who among that room full of strangers might be trusted; but now all the visitors to the zoo were cut off and his one big chance was gone. Only Ada lingered in the hall, and Ada was less than nobody at all. She was just a pair of worried eyes, and Danny already had a pair of his own.

"Do you think that was wise?" Laurent asked. "The boy did make a rather interesting proposition."

130

Beyond the door the murmurs were words, sharp and heated, and the glare Virgil bestowed upon Laurent would have scared the living daylights out of a lesser man.

"Real interesting," he agreed, "just like that proposition Trace made yesterday morning."

"But if the boy really knows something—"

"He can tell it to a judge!" Virgil snapped. "Tomorrow morning I'm taking Danny to Red Rock and turning him over to the district attorney. If you've got any squawk you can make it in court. Now how's about everybody clearing out of here so a man can get his supper?"

The badge on Virgil's shirt said he was the law, and when the law spoke, something should happen; but nobody was going to leave the office until Laurent left. Laurent was a bigger curiosity than Danny Ross, and it was obvious that the man had something on his mind. He moved toward the door and then turned back with a troubled frown.

"I hope you're prepared to give the prisoner adequate protection," he said.

"Don't you worry about that crowd outside," Virgil answered. "I can handle crowds."

"But can you handle assassins? Surely you realize, sheriff, that if Danny Ross really knows where to find that sheet of paper, and if that sheet of paper really does name Miss Allen's killer, then the boy's very existence is a deadly danger to someone."

"That's a couple of big 'ifs,'" Virgil said.

"Yes, I know. But I've known men to be hung on just one small 'if.' I should be very careful if I were you."

Alexander Laurent had reached the door by this time. He paused, surveyed the little group again, one by one, and went out smiling. It was an exit worthy of a star performer, and when Virgil's office drained of its unofficial visitors, he was not so alone as he wished to be. The doubt was still there, the nagging doubt so skillfully planted that one tiny word grew to huge dimensions. If. If Danny Ross really did know . . .

Virgil glared at the hall door, and his big hands tightened into fists. There was a way to make a kid like Danny talk— but only if you told him what to say. Truth was like water; it couldn't be held in a fist, and any chance of winning the kid's confidence had died the first time his knuckles met Danny's jaw. Smooth talk, that's what was needed, smooth talk and fancy words like those of Alexander Laurent; but Virgil's tongue had no magic, and his mind was as slow and methodical as a steam roller. The old anger rose up inside him like a banked furnace responding to a stoker. For all his strength, for all his pride of office, he wasn't a remarkable man. He was just a county sheriff, and he'd never be more than a county sheriff. A dumb county sheriff with a millstone of mistakes around his neck.

"Goddamit, don't just stand around with your fool mouth open!" he roared at the deputy. "Get outside and move that crowd along—and see that Jim Rice gets headed for home. I don't want any trouble from that hothead tonight."

Watching an underling scamper to carry out his orders brought Virgil's ego up a peg, but he was still uneasy. Damn Laurent anyway! Damn Ada and her nighttime wanderings! Damn that charred cabin in Peace Canyon! He had to do something with his fists, so he brought one down like a sledge hammer on the desk top. The gun Laurent had brought in danced to the accompaniment of the blow, reminding him of a simple truth. One shot had been fired, but the other chambers were filled. With a loaded gun in his hand Virgil felt better. He could even sit down and quietly contemplate the closed door to that cell block. The office afforded a good vantage point to a man on the alert.

"Ada!" he bellowed, and moments later the door pushed open a crack.

"I'll have my supper in here tonight."

Ada nodded absently.

"I'll have my pillow and blanket in here, too. And you keep that back door locked, you hear?"

"As you say, Virgil."

"And no walking out tonight!"

"No, Virgil, not tonight."

The door closed again, and she was gone, but Virgil's anger remained. He could shout at a deputy, he could shout at his wife; but he couldn't shout down the doubt. He walked over to the window and stared out at a street now emptied of human life. Cooperton was quieting down after a troubled day. The dusk had turned to darkness and the darkness to silence, and the only reminder of the day's fury was a pair of vehicles nosing the curbing in front of the Pioneer Hotel: a long gray sedan he'd seen at Laurent's ranch and a dusty red jeep. So they were still at it, those two. They were still cooking up schemes to make a fool of Virgil Keep!

"The way I look at it," Murph remarked, depositing a couple of beers beside the steaks Trace and Laurent were having in a rear booth of the bar, "nobody's ever going to know just what happened to Francy. Accident, murder—who can say? Francy sure can't, and nobody else is going to."

"The dead have been known to speak," Laurent murmured.

"Oh, I don't go for that spirit stuff! You live a while and then you die, that's it."

"I don't think Mr. Laurent was referring to spirits," Trace said. "You must know more about what goes on after hours than anybody else in town, Murph. Who would you say had the most reason for wanting Francy dead?"

"You mean outside of Trace Cooper?"

"I never wanted her dead."

"You should have. She played you for a sucker, Trace. She knew you were an easy touch."

"Never mind that!"

"O.K., O.K.!" Murph finished his chore and rubbed a restless hand over his bald dome. "I can think of a lot of wives who might have wanted her dead," he mused, "and I can think of one young lady who isn't a wife on account of Francy."

"Do you really believe a woman could have killed Francy?"

Murph shrugged. "Why not? Ain't you heard of equal rights? Anyway, it doesn't matter what I think, or what you think, or what Mr. Laurent thinks, because nobody's ever going to know what happened to Francy. Asking questions about that gal could stir up a lot of trouble for a lot of people, and it just ain't going to be stirred."

Murph delivered his judgment and sauntered back to the bar with an air of complete confidence. The weight of his words could not be denied. Despite the questionable circumstances of her death, Francy had been shoveled out of sight in an awful hurry—like the carcass of some stray cat that required no inquest and no mourning.

"The voice of the people," Trace observed. "How do we fight it?"

"With doubts," Laurent said.

"If you mean that 'any one of us could have done it' routine you don't know this town. That only draws everybody closer together."

"That's just the way we want them—close together. So close they're peering over each other's shoulders and reading each other's eyes." Laurent smiled over the rim of his beer glass. There was a kind of excitement in his eyes, like that of an old soldier returning to the wars. "The bartender's judgment on Miss Allen's death might well apply to the doctor's as well. Carrying the assumption further, we may see the force of public opinion acclaiming Mr. Malone the culprit of the crime as an easy out."

"But Malone's dead."

"By gunshot—quite a different method from the other deaths, as I pointed out to the sheriff a short while ago. If we are going to ignore Miss Allen's inkstained fingers and young Ross's illusive piece of paper, we must also ignore the motive for murdering Malone. We can then reach the conclusion that his death was the result of a drunken brawl by some person unknown and totally unrelated to the case at hand."

Trace could hardly believe his ears. "That's fantastic!" he protested.

"Not if properly presented to a carefully prepared jury. I assume you're still interested in defending Ross."

"Why not? He's innocent."

"Now we don't really know that, do we?"

"He didn't kill Malone!"

"I just told you how Malone was killed."

"Surely you don't expect me to believe that?"

"I do—if you're interested in saving Danny Ross. You must believe it. You must thoroughly convince yourself of an argument before you can convince a jury, Mr. Cooper."

Now Trace began to understand what Laurent was doing. He was outlining a way out if worst came to worst. The important thing was to save the innocent even if the guilty went free. The important thing was to find an alternative for Danny, even if that alternative never had a face or a name. For Laurent that might be enough, he had no score to settle, but Trace hadn't stayed sober this long for nothing.

"Malone might satisfy some people," he said, "but not me. Steve Malone didn't cause those bloodstains in that cabin!"

"But we have no bloodstains."

"We have Danny's eye witness story, and your son was there. He must have seen something."

"My son—" Laurent's face grayed before Trace's eyes, and he retreated into a momentary silence that had to give way to the inevitable. "You may as well know the worst before building up false hopes," he said. "My son will never make a witness for Danny Ross. By tomorrow, by the time Ross comes to trial of a certainty, he will have forgotten everything that happened in Peace Canyon today. He will have forgotten a cabin ever stood in that spot." Laurent spoke slowly, groping for words. "Douglas has a peculiar filter on his mind that strains out the unpleasant things. I don't know whether to pity or envy him."

Trace tried to understand what the old man was telling him. He fitted the words to the recollection of a boyish figure with an aging face, and the anguish in Laurent's eyes took on a name. "Then Douglas—" he began.

"Is perfectly rational! He's a child, Mr. Cooper, a strange child I only learned to know five years ago when his mother died and I was reminded of a life beyond the courtroom. He must not be brought into this affair! Can't you see what your fine townspeople would do to him? A stranger, an outsider—even more of an outsider than poor Danny Ross!"

Laurent's voice was quiet and intense, but his eyes were the eyes of an eagle. "Poor Danny Ross," he repeated. "That unfortunate little fool who always does the wrong thing at the very worst time. Now he sits in that cell like a clay pigeon at a shooting gallery, and your fine sheriff won't even listen to reason!"

Trace thought he was beginning to understand a few

things now: why a man gives up his career at the height of success, why he buries himself in a lonely desert. Laurent glanced nervously at the watch on his wrist. "I dislike being away from the ranch so long," he murmured. "Douglas isn't fond of the place, you know, and when he's upset his first instinct is to run away."

"But you do think Danny knows where to find that paper?" Trace asked.

"It's quite possible. It could happen just that way—some little thing remembered, some gesture or word. It isn't just what he knows that makes the lad's position so precarious; it's what everyone who heard his words thinks he knows." The frown on the old man's face made a deep ravine between his eyes. "What are you going to do about Danny Ross?" he demanded.

"What am *I* going to do?"

"You're the only one who can do anything. The sheriff won't listen to me, I'm an outsider too, but you—" A faint smile touched the corners of Laurent's mouth. "You are a Cooper. Oh, I've watched Virgil Keep's most expressive face this evening long enough to guess that his ancestors must have been lackeys to some ruling prince. He may hate your guts, Mr. Cooper, but he envies your blood. He'll listen to you."

"And if he does?"

"Then you get in to see Danny. Talk to him, reason with him. He was excited and frightened a little while ago, but he's had time now to calm down and face the facts. He must confide in someone, and you do have an honest face."

"And a stupid mind," Trace muttered.

"Not at all—a curious mind. That's why you'll never be satisfied with a hung jury even if it would set Danny free."

The truth of Alexander Laurent's words was as obvious as the cut of Trace's jaw. Doubt was no companion to live with. It was easy to shrug off the kid's challenge as a manifestation of hysteria; but did Danny Ross have the imagination to dream up such a bluff? He must have remembered something.

Trace could feel Laurent's eyes without looking at them. What was this turn all about anyway? What was the old boy

trying to prove? He didn't want to go back across the street
and argue with Virgil again—he'd carried this thing too far
already; but he couldn't very well refuse to co-operate as
long as he occupied the number-two spot for suspect of the
hour. That theoretical deathbed statement of Francy's was
his baby anyway. A man who dug up trouble should be
able to face it.

"All right," Trace sighed, "I'll go back to the lion's den
and see what I can do, but I don't think Virgil's going to be
very happy to see me. . . ."

Trace didn't have time to slide out of the booth before his
words turned sour. The bar of the Pioneer Hotel was virtu-
ally empty until the double doors to the lobby swung open.
The place seemed to get crowded with the sudden entrance
of just one man.

"Trace!" Virgil yelled. "Where's Trace Cooper?"

Virgil's face was beet red and his huge chest heaved as if
he'd just broken the record at the high hurdles. He looked
about wildly before that rear booth came into focus, and
then his expression changed to one of awe and bewilderment. "Mr. Laurent!" he gasped. "I thought you went with
him! I saw your car pulling away from the curb, and I
thought you went with him!"

"My car?" Laurent echoed. "What in the name of heaven
are you talking about?"

"Danny Ross. Somebody unlocked his cell door and
Danny's gone!"

Chapter Eighteen

Escaping from the Cooperton jail was easy; all that was
needed was a friend with a key to the cell door. Danny
didn't catch on to what was happening until after Ada's
third or fourth trip down the hall to Virgil's office. She
brought in a tray of supper; she brought back the empty
tray. She brought in an armful of bedding; she brought
back a frightened expression and something hidden under
the folds of her long apron. Danny was polishing off the

last of the meal she'd left him earlier. He might be on the brink of the scaffold, but his stomach didn't know it, and Ada was a wonderful cook.

"That was swell apple pie," he said. "I never ate such apple pie."

"Didn't you, Danny?" The woman's face brightened like a kid with a Christmas box. "Doesn't your mother make apple pies for you?"

"My mother works. She's got no time for making pies."

Danny could have bitten off his tongue for saying that. He wasn't supposed to have a mother, or any family at all, but Ada wasn't looking for inconsistencies in his story. She was just looking at Danny with a peculiar sort of sadness in her eyes.

"How old are you, Danny?" she asked.

"Eighteen," he said.

"Eighteen! I might have had a son eighteen . . . or is it twenty, or twenty-five? I can't seem to keep track of the years any more."

"What happened, did he die?"

Danny wasn't interested in the woman's memoirs; he was just making conversation. But the novelty of being encouraged was more than Ada could resist. "No, not that," she said. "I didn't have the baby, you see—it was a mistake. But I didn't know. I was frightened and I didn't know until after Virgil quit his schooling so's we could get married." She stopped talking abruptly, as if belatedly aware of hanging soiled linen on the line. But she didn't move away from the cell.

"Cages!" she said, glaring at the row of bars before her. "People shouldn't be kept in cages!"

"You can say that again!" Danny concurred.

"But we are—in one way or another."

Ada's hands were getting restless under the apron, and Danny caught a glimpse of metal that suddenly made this exchange of small talk the most interesting repartee in the world. The metal was a huge ring, and on that ring hung the keys to the cells. What she was leading up to he didn't dare to guess, but now he was a most attentive listener.

"But there's a way out, Danny. There's always a way out," she said. "Even I am getting out soon."

"Out of what?" Danny asked.

"My cage. I shouldn't tell you this, but when something really important happens to a person they have to tell someone. And you won't repeat it, will you?"

With that key on his mind Danny would have agreed to anything. "Not a word," he vowed.

"Because I don't want Virgil to know I'm going to die soon."

For a moment Danny forgot all about that key. "Die!" he echoed. "Where'd you get a crazy idea like that?" But it wasn't crazy, as he could see by taking a long look at her face. She was almost smiling, and her chin came up a little higher the way it had when she dropped the boom on Jim Rice.

"I know," she said firmly, "and Charley Gaynor knew, too, but he promised not to tell Virgil. Virgil would feel bad about the way he's treated me."

"Maybe he'd treat you better," Danny said.

"That's just it! He'd feel sorry and start being nice to me, and then when I'm gone he'd just remember how nice he was and forget all the mean things. I want him to remember!"

Danny didn't know why he trembled. It wasn't like seeing Virgil coming toward him with one of those big fists cocked. Anger he could understand, and a blow he could take, but such cold hatred as he glimpsed in Ada's eyes was enough to put a frost on the air. This mousy little woman, scampering at Virgil's beck and call—and all the time with her own terrible revenge simmering in her mind! This bit of understanding hit him like a cold shower, and then he got the big idea, the colossal idea that was going to get him out of that cell.

"He probably wouldn't believe you if you did tell him," he said. "He'd laugh at you. He'd tell you to shut up."

"He won't laugh," Ada insisted.

"Sure he will. That big ape hasn't got feelings enough to worry about anything. He's probably laughing at you right now because of what you said about Jim Rice and Francy. He probably thinks you made it all up."

"But I didn't!"

"Of course you didn't, no more than I made it up about

139

knowing what Malone did with that paper Francy signed. Wouldn't you like to see that paper, Mrs. Keep? Wouldn't you like for Virgil to come in here in the morning to get me and find you with that paper? Nobody'd laugh at you then. They'd all talk about how smart the sheriff's wife was to find the real murderer right under his nose!"

Danny had to be careful not to overdo this act. Ada might be slow but she wasn't simple.

"But I don't know where to find the paper," she said.

"I do. I saw Malone running for that bus, remember? I saw where he came from—" Danny stopped. He didn't want to blurt out everything until that door opened. "Let me out of here and I'll be back before morning," he promised.

It was Danny's big pitch, and he put all he had into it, so that he was a little off balance when Ada gave her answer. And she didn't give it with words, but with the scratching of the key turning in the lock. Then she smiled at him as if to say this was what she'd intended doing all the time.

"Run away, Danny Ross," she said. "Run fast as you can and don't come back. It doesn't matter about Francy, or the doctor, or about me—but you're just eighteen years old. Run away!"

She smiled at him, and Danny ran.

He could think about those things racing out to Mountain View. He had a high-powered car in hand and a head start on the sheriff, who'd seen him roar away from the curbing. Maybe Ada was right, and he should keep going, because there was nothing certain about that hunch of his, but it did seem strange that nobody had found the old doc's wallet in that search of the grounds. Malone wouldn't have kept it a minute longer than was needed to whip out that two hundred dollars, and the logical place for that business was inside the men's room just a few steps from where the old man hung his jacket on the spotlight. And then what? Was he likely to step outside in broad daylight with the wallet on him? With the hood up on the sedan Malone couldn't have known the doctor was already dead or dying; for all he knew he was poking in that jacket pocket for his missing wealth. Danny knew what he would have done, and that was good enough for a gamble when the odds were so long and the pay-off so big.

He was tired of running anyway. Running was a big joke, because life was going to get you wherever you went. It was going to hit you with one thing or hit you with another; but it sure as hell wasn't going to be easy and soft like the pictures in your daydreams. A cage, Ada said. Everybody lived in a cage, and maybe she was right. But a big cage was better than a little cage, and a risky life was better than no life at all.

The road was unfamiliar in the darkness. He slowed down for a crossing ahead, but it wasn't Mountain View. It was that narrow road winding down from Peace Canyon, the one he'd come over with Virgil a few hours earlier. By this time Danny knew what that crossing meant. It was where they had found Francy Allen with the life ebbing out of her. The place she'd been dumped for dead in the darkness. He had about five miles more to go, and about five minutes to plan what he'd do if this hunch turned sour.

Five minutes wasn't much time to pin a face on a murderer. The killer might be waiting for him at Mountain View with a shotgun again. He might be joining in the chase Virgil would have under way by now . . . or he might be a hundred miles away having a good laugh on everybody. But Danny didn't think so. Out here alone, with nothing but the road, and the moonlight, and a windshield spattered with stars, he could think clearly. Of all that talk back at the jail, one thing stood out. One lie that only Danny himself could catch. One lie could lead to another. . . .

And then he was scared, thinking maybe the killer had struck upon the same inspiration that was taking him back to where this whole grisly affair had started. Maybe he would be too late. But this time the crossing was Mountain View, and the cluster of faded yellow buildings was like a ghost town in the moonlight.

Walter and Viola must have gone to bed; there wasn't a light showing anywhere. Danny switched off the headlamps and let the motor ease to a whisper. A sweet-running job like this would be nice to have handy for a quick escape if worst came to worst. There was one obvious hiding place. He wheeled the sedan around to the far side of the old shed back of the café, and now he was conscious of a strange excitement much stronger than a hunch.

There were times when something was done that seemed to have been done before. That was a moon riding high in the sky now instead of the sun, and there was no aging sedan rattling down the highway from Red Rock. But everything was familiar; everything was plain. Danny crawled out from under the steering wheel and came cautiously around the end of the shed. A few feet ahead was the spot where old Doc Gaynor had parked his ailing vehicle, and a few steps beyond was the door of the men's room. A company station would have locked up for the night, but the only lock on that door was the rusty bolt inside that Danny slid home when he went in. He listened to the night sounds for a few long moments before switching on the naked bulb over the lavatory. A light was risky but necessary. If Malone actually had left the doctor's wallet in the men's room, any risk was justified. If he hadn't, it would take more than darkness to cover Danny now.

But where, in this tiny cubicle, would a thief hide the evidence of his theft? A loose floor board? A crack in the wall? A high shelf? In his anxiety, Danny kicked over the waste basket and then held his breath when the phone began ringing inside the café. That would be someone in Cooperton calling to warn Walter of a big gray sedan barreling north. He could even catch the low rumble of a sleepy voice on the other side of the thin partition.

But where could Malone have dropped the wallet? It was time to douse the light and run, but Danny couldn't make himself give up the search. Giving up meant running and being hunted again, and the wallet had to be here! Charley Gaynor's killer hadn't found it. Why else was Malone dead? . . . There was only one place left to look when he heard the siren screaming up the highway, and then the shriek of brakes and the flail of gravel on the drive. A barrage of headlights hit the side of the building just as Danny switched off the bulb.

"Come on out, Danny! Come out with your hands up or I'll start shooting!"

That was Virgil's baritone bawling at the bolted door, but he wasn't alone. It sounded like a parade turning off onto the gravel. "Better come out, Danny," Trace called, and then Viola began a shrill demand to know what was going on, what was all the excitement. How many more? Danny stood on tiptoe and peeked through the tiny window. He could see them all swarming before the headlights like a convention of moths at a lamppost, only this time it wasn't the moths who were going to get burned. The party was complete—nobody missing. No body and no thing, because the last place to look had been the right place. Danny had heard about the man who brought his harp to the party and nobody asked him to play, but here he was with an eager audience and a harp without strings. There was only one chance. . . .

"Save the fireworks!" he yelled. "I'm coming out! I'm coming out with the wallet!"

It was like ground zero the moment before an A-bomb test. The silence could have been boxed up and wrapped for mailing. With one hand Danny reached up and unscrewed the light bulb. It was still hot, but not nearly so hot as that limp leather fold in his other hand. "Stand away from the door! I'm coming out!" he cried, and at the instant the door flew open the bulb hit the cement floor like a pistol shot.

Fire at random into a crowd of spectators and everybody scampers—that's what Danny counted on and that's what he got. Just a moment of confusion, a precious moment for a head start, and he was off for the sedan like an all-American back heading for pay dirt. He wasn't sure if there were footsteps behind him, beside him, or ahead of him. He wasn't sure if there was shouting, or if the only sound was the pounding of his own heart. The shed, that's all he could think of—the far side of the shed and a gray sedan waiting in the moonlight. But he hadn't counted on a chauffeur.

When the car door swung open in his face, Danny tried to reverse his field; but there was no escaping the hand that dragged him into the front seat, and no crying out against the roar of the motor as the sedan leaped into motion. At the crossing the car swung left. The unpaved side road rushed up to meet them like a narrow tunnel opening in the moonlight, and there was only a cloud of dust for the watchers behind. . . . There were times when something was done that seemed to have been done before.

"You knew where to look for the car all right," Danny said. "It must have been a long wait for the old doc to show up the other day . . . and with a passenger yet!"

Danny was a long way from being as calm as he tried to sound, and he wasn't going to get any response while the pursuing headlights showed dimly through the dust in the rear-view mirror. But all those horses under the hood were paying off. The lights grew smaller by the second.

"What happens to me now? A bullet in the head like Malone?"

"Don't be a fool!" Laurent answered. "All I want is that piece of paper."

Alexander Laurent's face was like a white mask in the moonlight, and his eyes never left that tortuous road they were using for a speedway. "A piece of paper," he repeated, "that contains nothing but a hideous lie. Surely you don't want to convict an innocent man, Danny. You know what it is to be falsely accused."

"I don't know what you mean," Danny began.

"Of course you don't. You never knew Francy Allen."

Laurent hit the brakes, but only long enough to make the turnoff to the ranch. Danny recognized the place from the morning he'd watched the jeep swing out of sight and leave him alone with Virgil Keep. It had been a lonely feeling, but nothing like the feeling he had now. There were no lights left in the rear view, and Laurent went on talking as if they had been sitting in somebody's living room swapping yarns before the fire.

"She was an evil woman, Danny. A vindictive woman. She wrecked Trace Cooper's happiness with a lie because he didn't love her, and she would have destroyed my son with another."

"If he hadn't destroyed her first," Danny said.

"No! You're wrong, Danny! That statement is a lie!"

Now Danny knew what he hadn't known before, and being scared wasn't so bad when someone else was scared along with him. "The only lie I know about is the one you told the sheriff," he said. "Douglas didn't fire that gun

144

when I threw the clothes at him, and when he did, he wasn't shooting at any lamp. He was shooting at me!"

"Because he was excited—"

"Excited enough to set fire to a cabin full of bloodstains!"

Danny saw Laurent's long fingers tighten on the steering wheel, but the mask didn't change. "Listen to me, Danny," he said quietly. "Listen and try to understand. You think that you've learned the truth at last, but you're wrong. The truth is much uglier than it seems. Francy Allen used that cabin for her rendezvous with Jim Rice, and my son knew it. He watched Rice leave that last night, and then went in and ordered her off the premises—much as he ordered you off this afternoon."

"But with a skillet instead of a gun," Danny muttered.

"No, not with a skillet or a gun! He simply told her to leave, and she flew into a rage. She hated him, Danny. She would have hated anyone who occupied what she still considered her rightful home. Perhaps, in that twisted mind of hers, she even thought me responsible for Cooper's losing the ranch and wanted to strike at me through Douglas. Whatever her reasons, she defied Douglas to put her out. She told him she would use that cabin whenever she pleased. She said she would accuse him of attacking her if he interfered again!"

Laurent seemed to choke on his own words. For the first time the great voice faltered.

"Oh, she was clever!" he added. "She could see that Douglas was different. Not just a stranger, Danny, as you were when they threw you in that cell, but a poor unfortunate the wagging tongues of Cooperton could destroy with such a charge."

"A nut," Danny said, and the old man's lips trembled in the moonlight.

"In your vocabulary, perhaps. Nevertheless, he's innocent of Francy Allen's murder. She was alive when he left the cabin. Why, Douglas doesn't even know that the woman is dead! Setting fire to the cabin was just his way of disposing of something ugly and troublesome!"

And dangerous, Danny thought. But he didn't want to challenge Laurent yet. The important thing was to keep him talking. And there was always a chance he was telling the truth. That was the trouble with life; every once in a while somebody told the truth and got a guy all confused. "I must have that statement," Laurent said again, and Danny clutched the leather wallet all the tighter.

"And what happens to me if I give it to you?"

"Nothing. You can let me off at the ranch and take my car."

"And run for the rest of my life?"

"You don't have to run. Give yourself up and face the charge. I've been working to save you from the very beginning, Danny, and I've yet to lose a capital case."

That did it. Up to a point Danny was just a pair of ears listening to a gifted persuader, but suddenly the voice lost its persuasion and the truth stood out ugly and naked. A capital case! That's all Danny Ross meant to Alexander Laurent. It was a little hard to take after all these years of thinking he was a human being with feelings and rights. And if that's all he was, what was old Doc Gaynor? What was a little man in a wrinkled raincoat?

Danny shivered. They were all alone in a moon-bathed desert, with the night air rushing in through the open window behind Laurent's shoulder, and a dark shadow beginning to take form up ahead. The shadow would be the trees at the edge of the ranch-house grounds—the only possible shelter, he suddenly realized, in all this wide loneliness. Trees, and an open window. He bit back his words until the time was right. Funny how these brainy guys who wanted to do everybody's thinking always overlooked little details like open windows. . . .

"So you've been working to save me!" Danny said at last. "Now I'll tell one! You only sent Cooper to the jail to get a line on that wallet you didn't find in the old doc's pocket."

"Don't be a fool!" Laurent gasped.

"That's just what I'm not being any more! You're trying to make me believe Francy Allen put the finger on Douglas on her deathbed and it was all a lie!"

"She didn't know it was a lie. She was struck from behind."

"You seem to know a lot about what happened in that cabin."

"Douglas told me."

"You don't say!"

Danny paused. The trees were looming large now. He couldn't wait much longer.

"And did Douglas tell you what was in Francy's statement?" he asked.

It was almost funny to see Laurent change. One minute he was the Great White Father, full of warmth and kindness, and the next he was just a desperate man with a forty-five in one hand and sudden death in his eyes.

"I'll take that wallet now," he said.

"Is that what you told the old doc?"

"Doctor Gaynor was a fool! He knew Douglas' condition. He believed what that woman told him."

"And what did Malone believe?"

"Malone?" Laurent seemed to have trouble recalling anyone so insignificant. "How could I be sure Malone hadn't read the statement and would remember when his drunken stupor wore off? Good God, Danny, I didn't want to kill those men! But that woman reached beyond the grave to destroy my son! I had no choice!"

No choice was exactly what Danny had at the moment. No choice, and the old man's wallet held high so Laurent could get a good look at it. It could mean a bullet in the belly or a bullet in the back—no choice.

"Go ahead and shoot!" he bellowed, "but you'll still need this!" The wallet sailed through the open window into darkness.

When Laurent hit the brakes, Danny hit the dirt. The first shot went wild, and then the old man had to go back and retrieve that precious wallet. Time enough then for Danny to reach the shelter of the trees, a shelter that was both friend and traitor. Every crackling branch, every broken twig cried out directions to a desperate old man beyond caution who fired at random and then stood motionless in the moonlit clearing, waiting for the next telltale sound.

For what seemed a very long time, no sound came. Crouched behind a stunted bush, Danny watched and barely dared to breathe. It was all picture-clear in the moonlight—Laurent poised like some silver-crowned executioner, and a few yards away the gray sedan with its long radio aerial pointing like a slender spear toward the stars.

147

Danny remembered that dry riverbank and the car heading south toward Junction City, and then he remembered that car in the alley behind a run-down hotel. He knew all the answers now, except where he was going when Laurent came toward him.

But that was an answer he never had to find. He might have caught the sound sooner if the footsteps behind him hadn't been in tempo with his own pounding heart. He might have cried out a warning if there had been time. But the time had all run out and the shadows and sounds had no names now. Laurent whirled and fired once more. One shot, one cry, and then the long silence. . . .

Danny didn't emerge from his hiding place until Virgil and all the others swarmed over the scene. A short distance away Alexander Laurent sat on the ground stroking his dead son's hair. The gun was forgotten on the earth beside him; he had no use for it now. He had no use for the sheriff and his party, and no ears for Danny's frantic story. He had been oblivious to every sound and movement since that cry of anguish when Douglas stumbled out of the shadows to fall at his feet, and not until Virgil found the wallet did he return to life.

"It's all a lie!" he cried out. "I killed that Jezebel! Everything on that paper is a lie!"

Danny almost felt sorry for the old man when Virgil ripped open the wallet. Two and a half days in the flush tank hadn't left enough ink on Francy's statement to tell any tales on anyone.

Chapter Nineteen

Murder was an untidy business. When Douglas, drawn by the sound of gunfire and his own nameless terror, ran into the blaze of his father's gun, the world ended for Alexander Laurent; but the debris of murder still had to be cleared away. A regiment of questions had to be reviewed like troops marching single file, and for that purpose the lights burned late in the sheriff's station at Cooperton.

"For a man who was always such a big talker," Virgil said

later, "it was like pulling back teeth to get the full story out of him."

"Or having a dead man recite his own obituary," Trace suggested.

"And what an obituary! I think the old guy's as nutty as his son, at least on one subject. He quit his practice just so he could get Douglas away from people. He knew the boy was dangerous! He even followed him around like a damned nursemaid!"

"Even to Peace Canyon in the dark of night," Trace murmured.

"That's the trouble; he followed him there once too often and heard Francy's threat. After that her life wasn't worth a nickel!"

Virgil leaned back in the creaky swivel chair behind his desk and rubbed his face with both hands. It was getting on toward midday, and he was missing the sleep all that questioning had stolen. After the confession there had been the long morning ride to Red Rock and back, and then the phone calls to Junction City, and the statements to a press that had just discovered a black dot on the map named Cooperton. He was beginning to wish Charley Gaynor had given Laurent the statement and saved all this trouble—a strange thought for a man who lived so by the law that many wondered how he would know right from wrong if it wasn't written down.

When Virgil looked up again, Trace was still standing beside the desk. "Exit Francy," he said. "The rest I can imagine."

"I'll bet you can! Do you want to know how Laurent got to Malone? It was easy with the right kind of help. When Francy didn't die soon enough he got worried; after all, Douglas was the only uninvited guest she saw that night. So he drove down to Mountain View to get to Charley before Charley got to me, killed him when he refused to destroy that statement, and then discovered that a pickpocket had beaten him to it. That's when Laurent put on his thinking cap. If he came asking after Danny Ross, I might get suspicious, but some people just naturally fall for fancy language."

"Is this my biography?" Trace inquired.

149

"With pictures! What did he do when you told him about Danny's man in a raincoat?"

"Sent me to Junction City to look for him."

"Exactly. And then he took the other road down, knowing the road block wasn't alerted for an old man in a gray sedan, and had no trouble at all spotting that red jeep of yours. That left you to do the questioning and leave the trail." Virgil paused significantly and then put into words what Trace was thinking. "Who knows? If you'd actually reached Malone first Fisher might be planning a funeral for you."

"I knew all the time there was something queer about Laurent," Danny chimed in. "No expensive lawyer gives away free samples."

It was a little mean of Danny to add to Trace's discomfort, especially when Trace was the reason he was outside of a cell and not wanted by the law for the first time in three days. Virgil, remembering that pistol blow on his head and the sedan that was even now being hauled out of the dry river bed, was dead set against release; but Trace fixed that. "My client," he said (sounding as if he'd written the book), "may have a few complaints of his own. False arrest, imprisonment without formal charge, police brutality—" Right about then Virgil decided to be generous, and that was why Danny was gathering up his possessions. He had the canvas zipper bag under his arm, an old jacket of Trace's to replace the one lost in the fire, and a tight wad of bills in his levis. Two hundred dollars, just like when he'd hit town.

"I suppose now you'll be telling us that you knew Laurent was guilty all along," Trace said.

"I didn't say that," Danny protested. "I thought it was Malone until he turned up dead. After that I was too busy to think. I didn't wise up until Laurent started giving me that big pitch in the car last night. I got to remembering something the old doc said when I was riding with him, something about needing another language to say what he didn't like to say. I figured it must have been Laurent he was talking about, and what he'd have to tell him about his son. And how could Laurent be so sure of what was in that statement if the doc hadn't told him?"

"While you were finishing a Coke," Trace muttered.

Trace didn't like to talk about it. The whole affair made him both sad and angry—sad because death was sad, and angry because he'd been played for a sucker all around. By Francy, by Jim Rice, but most of all by Alexander Laurent. Perhaps his score with Laurent had been settled when Douglas fell before his father's eyes; but being used for a stooge wasn't a pleasant experience even when it came under the guise of benevolence. *Noblesse oblige!* Now that the idol had fallen, Trace could see the flaws in the clay. Laurent's world was filled with Douglases—childlike creatures to be protected, tolerated, and even used if necessary, but never allowed to mature to their own stature. The Great White Father bestowing life and death as he saw fit!

When Arthur suddenly appeared in the street doorway, Trace spun about and pointed a finger at him. "Where would you be without me?" he challenged.

Arthur didn't seem particularly impressed. "Are you kidding?" he asked. "Without you I'd be getting some work done. We've got a barn roof that needs fixing and—"

"You're damned right you would!" Trace broke in. "And I'll tell you something else. All the people here in town, and the ones outside town, would be doing just exactly what they're doing now if there'd never been a Cooper on God's good earth. Laurent's welcome to that pile of rocks my ancestors built. He's even welcome to my ancestors—and he may be seeing some of them soon. Let's get at that roof!"

Trace was having such a good time with his self-discovery, he didn't even notice the telegram Arthur had brought until it was shoved under his nose. He turned his back on Virgil and read it quickly. It was the answer to the one sent from Red Rock the day before, a confirmation actually. But now that he had it, what was he to do? A man likes to make his own decisions, good or bad, and Danny had certainly earned the right.

He looked up and saw the kid turning toward the door. "What's your hurry?" he asked.

"I see a bus coming in," Danny said.

It was an understatement. Roads and old motors being what they were, transportation usually came to Cooperton in bunches or not at all. Two busses were pulling up in front of the depot across the street, one heading north and one heading south, and Danny hadn't mentioned his destination.

"It's not that I don't appreciate the hospitality," he added, "but I have a sort of a date. Here—" He hauled the language dictionary out of his pocket and tossed it on Virgil's desk. "You keep this," he said. "You might need it."

It was too late to stop him then. Throwing Trace and Arthur a broad wink, Danny sauntered across the street, tall and lanky in his tight levis and with the sun making a golden crown of his stubby hair. For a moment they lost sight of him behind the busses, and then the southbound pulled out and he waved just once before climbing aboard the other.

As soon as they were out of Virgil's office, Trace made a tight wad of the telegram in his hand. "I think we should wire Danny's draft board to keep their shirts on," he said, "and say he's on his way."

"Via the scenic route?" Arthur suggested.

"No . . ."

With the busses out of the way, Trace could see something else in the line of unfinished business. Joyce was just turning in at the drugstore across the street, and he tried to remember the last time he'd bought a girl a drink at a fountain.

"Let's just say the kid hit a detour," he concluded. "It happens to the best and the worst of us."

BLACK LIZARD BOOKS